# Spring Break in Calabasas with A Gangsta

## J'Ann Marie

# *Rhymedi*

*Bitter*

*Mad at me, mad at my nigga*

*Mad at the fact he ain't wit cha*

*Mad at the fact that it's me*

*But this shit bigger...*

My cousin Brittani and I sang along to Summer Walker's "Bitter" as she re-twisted and styled my bright red dreadlocks. It was a Saturday afternoon, and we both had an off day, so we used it to get this nappy head of mine together. I was tired of looking in the mirror at all of my new growth.

"Girl, Summer came with it on this album!" Brittani stated as she twirled one of my locs between the palm of her hands.

"Didn't she, though?!" I agreed. "I've always loved Summer's music." I snapped my fingers and bobbed my head to the beat.

"I mean, I have too, but this album is on a whole 'nother level."

"That's what happens when a fuck nigga breaks your heart." I smacked my lips and rolled my eyes. Just saying those few words put a damper on my mood as I dwelled on my past relationship.

"Yeah, that and when you have talent. That girl Summer has some serious skills," Brittani snickered.

"She really does, though," I seconded her comment. "Hell, I wish I had those skills. I could've wrote a hell of a song about my relationship with Terry," I scoffed, shaking my head.

"Fuck a song, you could write a whole album and then some about his bitch ass! AND get a Grammy off that muthafucka," Brittani spat, frowning her face in disgust. "Ooh, I can't stand that nigga! Why you even bring his name up?" she then questioned.

"I don't know. Listening to this album just always make me think about him," I shrugged. "I mean, not the whole album, but a few songs."

"I just wish you could turn your brain off from thinking about his ass at all," she replied, applying twisting gel to the next loc she was about to twist.

Sighing heavily, I smacked my lips. "Shit, me too. But the shit is easier said than done. I can at least say the shit gets easier as the days go by," I replied.

"Yeah well, I'm happy to hear that. That clown doesn't deserve to occupy any space in your brain," she told me. "Fuckin' inconsiderate bastard." She then added just above a whisper, causing me to snicker.

Terry was my ex fiancé, and Brittani hated his ass. I couldn't say I blamed her though; the nigga had done me beyond dirty. Together for four years, our relationship was perfect. He was my soulmate and I was his. We had one of those bonds people dreamed to have with their mate; we were inseparable.

On our three year relationship anniversary, Terry proposed and asked me to become his wife. I was on cloud nine because all I ever wanted was to build a life and family with him. That same night, my life changed forever. On the way home from the proposal dinner, Terry and I were in a bad car accident. He managed to walk away without a scratch; I, on the other hand, wasn't so lucky.

Suffering from major spinal damage, I lost mobility in my lower extremities and was confined to a wheelchair for life. The pain I felt in my heart when the doctors told me that I would never walk again was indescribable. I wanted to die right then and there. I didn't know how I was going to live stuck in a chair when I was used to a living life freely. I spent months questioning God's plan. I was only twenty-six, and my whole life had been stripped away from me.

The first six months of being a paraplegic was the worst. Though Terry stuck around, he would always complain about all of the things he had to do for me. That shit only made me feel worse because it wasn't like I'd asked to be this way. Still, I sucked up the mean things he'd say because I didn't want to be alone. Not only that, but no other man was going to want a disabled girl — at least, that's what Terry would say.  I didn't have the options to complain when I was the one who needed help.

I was so ashamed of being in a chair that I refused to leave home. If I wasn't going to the doctor, I wasn't going anywhere. I didn't even attend family functions. If anyone wanted to see me, they would have to come to my house. If I needed to shop for groceries, household supplies, or anything, I would do it all online. I was a consultant for AT&T, and I even worked from home. I closed myself off from the rest of the world, and I liked it that way. I didn't have to worry about people staring at me or hear the low whispering when I entered a room. The shit was draining.

You would think Terry had a problem with that, but he didn't. It wasn't like he wanted to be seen in public with me anymore, anyway. When I got in the chair, everything he did to make me smile stopped. Date nights, random gifts, affection, sex – it was all a thing of the past. Hell, we didn't even sleep in the same bed together. Terry would say it was because he slept wild and was scared to hurt me in his sleep but deep down, I knew otherwise. It was clear his feelings for me weren't the same and as much as it hurt, there was nothing I could do about it.

One day, Terry left for the store and never returned. A couple of days later, Brittani ran into him at the mall with another girl. According to her, they were holding hands and smiling like they were in love. Long story short, she beat up him and the chick while our other cousin, Alicia, recorded it. That same week, Brittani moved in and had been caring for me ever since. I thanked God for her every day because if it wasn't for her and my parents, I would've given up a long time ago.

"Anyway, on a lighter note," Brittani sighed, changing the subject. You remember Havoc? The guy I've been talking to?" she asked.

"You mean the nigga you met on Facebook?" I turned, giving her the side eye.

"Uh uhn, don't do that," Brittani smacked her lips.

"What? I'm just saying, you did meet him on Facebook, right?"

"Uh yeah, but that's beside the point, Rhym!" she snapped.

Letting out a deep sigh, I bit my tongue. "Okay, cuz, I apologize. "What about him?" I then asked dryly.

"Thank you," she spat. "Anyway, like I was saying, he invited me to his beach house in Calabasas for his birthday. And since it's Spring Break and all, I was thinking, maybe we should go," she finished.

Scoffing, I quickly turned to face her. "Hell you mean, WE?" I asked, placing emphasis on the word. "I know yo' ass ain't speaking French now."

"Come on, cuz, don't do me like that," she pouted, but that shit didn't move me one bit.

"Nah, don't do yourself like that. You know damn well I won't even go to the corner store, let alone fuckin' California, with some nigga you barely even know."

"Come on, Rhym, please! I would do it for you," she begged. "Plus, Alicia and Monica coming too," she added.

"Well, there you go. If they're going, you don't need me!" I told her.

"Wow, really, Rhymedi?"

"Really! If they're going, why do you need me?" I questioned.

I wasn't trying to be mean, but Brittani knew how I felt about leaving the house to even go up the street. So for her to ask me to leave the state was insane.

"Rhymedi, it's only for a weekend!" she stated as if it was supposed to change my mind. "Plus, you know how I feel about you. Since Pampers, it's just been you and me. You let that chair get in the way, but I don't give a fuck about none of that; you're still the same old Rhym to me. And as long as you have breath in your body, I'm going to make sure you live life to the fullest. Now please," she stated sincerely, but I still wasn't budging.

"Brittani! I don't care if it was only for a day, I don't wanna go! You know how I feel about being in public. So for you to even ask me to go is fucked up."

Brittani scoffed and rolled her eyes in disappointment. "No, what's fucked up is you not living your life and letting this chair get the best of you!" she pouted, kicking the wheel of my chair.

"Kick my fuckin' chair again!" I spat, rolling my eyes.

Like the asshole she was, Brittani kicked my chair harder than the first time. "I don't give a fuck about your little threats. I'm sick of yo' ass!" she spat. "You can't spend the rest of your life cooped up in this fuckin' apartment, you know that, right?" she then asked.

"Says who?" I shot back.

"Says fuckin' me!" she walked around to the front of me. Kneeling down, she stared me square in the eyes. "You're young, beautiful as fuck, and you still have a long life ahead of you, Rhymedi. I'll be so happy when you finally realize that," she finished.

Sighing, I darted my eyes towards the floor. I appreciated my cousin for looking out for me and always stroking my ego, but I knew she was only saying those things because she loved me. No matter how good she tried to make me feel, I saw myself as just another helpless soul.

## *Homicide*

My little brother, Havoc, and I stepped down the steps of our private jet as the bright ass L.A. sun beamed off the diamond Cubans around our necks, damn near blinding us. Cupping my hand over my eyes, I tried my best to block that shit, but it wasn't working. We'd just touched back down from doing some business in Colorado, and it was safe to say that we would be opening another weed farm in Denver. Excited was an understatement for the way we were feeling. It was our fifth out of state location, and the money was flowing in like water — legal money at that! Our goal was to eventually grace all fifty states.

"What you 'bout to get on, fool?" Havoc asked as we made our way to our rides.

"Shit, 'bout to go home to my bitch. A nigga need to bust a NUT!" I laughed, pointing the key fob towards my ride and popping the trunk. I then threw my duffle bag inside.

"See, if you was living wild and free like me, you wouldn't have that problem. I bussed so many nuts in Denver, a nigga lost count," he bragged like that shit was good.

"Yeah, and I bet you lost count of the bitches too, huh?"

"You know it," he chortled.

"My nigga!" I laughed and stuck my hand out for some dap. When he was about to pound me up, I snatched my fist away and straight faced his ass. "Fuck on, ole dumb ass. You need to stop doing that shit before your fuckin' dick fall off, dummy!" I then spat.

Sucking his teeth, Havoc waved me off. "Shut up, bitch boy! You just mad 'cause Ariel's ole boujee ass got a leash around yo' neck, and you can't have no more fun. Ole pussy whipped ass!" He made a whip sound and motioned his arm as if he was whipping something.

"Nigga, fuck you!" I couldn't help but snicker. "Ain't nobody got shit whipped; I'm just done fuckin' off. There's more to life than just rotating women. I've finally found my person, and I'm fuckin' with her," I shrugged.

"I finally found my person, and I'm fuckin with her," he mocked, making funny faces. "Man, what the fuck ever! Fuck on with that bullshit!" he then sucked his teeth. "Besides, you already know how I feel about Ariel's biscuit head ass."

"Yeah, I do. So shut the fuck up!" I grimaced, shooting him an evil glare.

I didn't even want him to start talking about Ariel because once he started, his ass wasn't going to stop. On top of that, I wasn't in the mood to hear the shit. I was tired of him telling me how much he couldn't stand my bitch and how she wasn't right for me. Let him tell it, we didn't have shit in common, and I was sprung off a fat ass and a smile.

"Yeah ok, nigga. One day, you gon' look back on these times and thank me for telling you that bitch ain't shit."

"Aye nigga, watch yo' fuckin' mouth! And I keep telling you, don't worry about my shit. You just better hope you find somebody that wanna put up with yo' arrogant ass for the rest of they life," I told him.

"Man, fuck you, boy! I done already found my wife."

"Yeah, right. Nigga, who?" I asked, knowing his ass was all cap.

"Her name Brittani, she bad as fuck too." He licked his lips, rubbing his hands together like Birdman.

Smacking my teeth, I chortled hard as fuck. "Man, fuck on! You talking about that chick you met on IG?" I inquired.

"Facebook, bitch," he quickly corrected me.

"Shit, that's even worse."

"Fuck you!" Havoc sucked his teeth, causing me to bust another chuckle.

"Damn nigga, why so hostile towards me? I'm just saying. I've known you to do a lot of crazy ass shit, but dating hoes off social media ain't one of them—especially when you got bitches falling at yo' feet on a daily."

"Okay, and?! It's 20 fuckin' 22; social media is the way of the world. Ain't shit wrong with meeting a hoe on there."

"Yeah well, fuck that. I ain't fuckin' with it."

"That's why my name Havoc and yours Homicide, the fuck," he grimaced.

"You damn right. Ole sick ass," I turned my nose up at him. "You don't know who the fuck you talking to behind that fuckin' computer. It could be a fuckin' transvestite! You gon' go meet that bitch, and she might have more dick than you." I fell out laughing but was serious as a heart attack. "You better watch *Catfish*, boy. This shit ain't no game," I then told him.

"Nigga, I'd shoot that muthafucka then come and shoot yo' ass for burning bread. Stop playing with me, Loyal," he grimaced, calling me by my government name.

Laughing, I threw my hands up in surrender. "Aight, bro, I'm just fucking with you. But on some real shit, be careful with that shit. It's wicked out here."

"And so am I. Muthafuckas know better than to play with me, man. I'll make they ass the headline of a news article QUICK!"

"Already!" I chortled, dapping him up. "Well, for yo' sake, I hope this Brittani chick don't have a dick."

"You know what? I'm out. Gone on home to that ole pie face bitch you call a fiancée," Havoc snapped, opening the driver's door to his army green, 2021 Dodge Durango 392.

"At least I know for a fact she's all woman." I flipped him the bird before hopping in my smoked gray 2021 wide body Hellcat Charger.

Cranking my engine, I revved it up as my little brother did the same. Skirting off, we raced through traffic until going our separate ways. About twenty minutes later, I was pulling into the roundabout driveway of me and Ariel's home. A smile graced my face when I noticed her G-Wagon parked outside of one of our three garage doors. I missed my baby, and I couldn't wait to hug and kiss her.

Killing the ignition, I hopped out and grabbed my bags before making my way inside. Upon entering the threshold, I was caught by surprise when I noticed our housekeeper, Esmerelda, stacking luggage by the doorway. Raising my brow in curiosity, I dropped my bags right where I stood.

"What's good, Esmerelda? What the fuck is this?" I asked, motioning my head towards the things. I didn't mean to come off so hostile, but I was muddled as fuck.

"Hi, Mr. Taylor," she sighed, out of breath. "I'm sorry, but I'm only doing what Ms. Harris asked me to do. I don't know," she shrugged with a puzzled look, speaking her best English.

An illegal immigrant from Puerto Rico, Esmerelda had been working for me for going on four years; she was like family. She held my home front down, and in return, I paid her a nice, hefty salary. Her sister, Enya, even worked for Havoc. I believed his hoe ass was fucking her, but that was another story for a different day.

"Wait, what? Ari got you doing this?" I questioned, being sure I'd heard her correctly.

"Yes sir. She asked me to be finished before you got here but —," she huffed, throwing her hands up in defeat. "¡Mierda, Mierda, maldita sea! She's going to be so mad." Esmerelda ran her hands through her charcoal black hair, cursing in a panic. I didn't know what the fuck I'd walked in on, but I was about to get to the bottom of it.

"Aye, just calm down and take a deep breath," I placed my hands on her shoulders, looking her in the eyes. Doing as I asked, Esmerelda inhaled deeply, before slowly letting it out. When she was all the way calm, I continued to speak.

"I want you to listen to me and listen to me good. It is me who signs your fuckin' check every Friday, so you shouldn't give two fucks about how she feels."

"Yes sir," she nodded, repeatedly.

"Now I'm going to go find Ariel and see what the fuck is up. You go prepare dinner or something. Leave this shit right where it's at," I demanded.

"Yes sir," she smiled. "And welcome home, Mr. Taylor. I'm so glad you're back." Esmerelda then took off down the long hallway toward the kitchen.

I made my way towards the stairs and took them by two, up to our bedroom. Letting myself into the closed double doors, I found Ariel stuffing clothes into more suitcases. I stood there for a moment, sucking my teeth as I tried to wrap my mind around the situation. Right before leaving for Colorado, shit was all good. So I couldn't understand what had happened between then and now, that had her packing up, ready to leave a nigga.

"Damn, you got somewhere to be?" Ariel flinched like a battered child at the sound of my voice.

She was so caught up in what she was doing, she hadn't even noticed that I'd entered the room. When her eyes landed on me, it looked as if she'd run into her karma.

"L-Loyal, heeey," she let out a fake ass chuckle while grasping her chest. "You scared me; I thought you weren't coming back in town until tomorrow."

"Good thing I didn't, I wouldn't have walked in on this." I pointed towards the luggage. "What's the deal, Ariel? Where you going?" I slowly walked in her direction.

Blinking repeatedly, Ariel cleared her throat as she tucked her bone straight tresses behind her left ear. "Uhm, see, that's what I wanted to talk to you about." Her ass was looking everywhere but at me as she fidgeted with freshly manicured nails. It was the shit she did when she was being untruthful.

"Aw yeah," I chuckled at her lying ass. "When were you planning to do that? 'Cause it looks to me you were about to just leave and let a nigga come back to an empty house. And according to Esmerelda, she was supposed to be done loading your truck before I returned." I stared her down with menacing eyes.

"That bitch," Ariel muttered through gritted teeth. "Well then, there you go," she then shrugged carelessly.

"Fuck you mean, there I go? What the fuck is up, Ariel?" I got in her face, demanding an explanation.

"Look, Loyal," she sighed. "I'm leaving you. I didn't want to tell you and hurt your feelings, since you just recently proposed and all," she rolled her eyes to the top of her head. "But this just isn't working for me anymore. I'm sorry."

Ariel went to tuck her hair behind her ear again, and that's when I noticed an engagement ring on her finger, but it wasn't the one I'd gotten her. Feeling my heart rate increase, my ears grew hot as I snatched her by the wrist and held her left hand up.

"Fuck is this shit, Ari?" I questioned with flared nostrils.

Sighing heavily, she rolled her eyes and yanked her hand away. "It's the reason I'm leaving you. I'm marrying someone else, Loyal," she spat, stinging the fuck out of my heart.

Scoffing, I ran my hand over my face before taking a seat on the edge of the bed. I needed a minute to grasp what she'd just said. I was praying my ears were deceiving me, but looking at the clothes stuffed in the suitcases before me, I knew it was true.

All I could think was how? Not only that, but why? I had been nothing short of amazing to Ariel the whole three years we'd been together. I mean, we had our ups and downs, but the shit was minor compared to the shit most couples went through. I'd never cheated on her, let alone given her a reason to think I was. Just like my name, I was loyal. Apparently, she couldn't say the same, considering she was already engaged to be married to another nigga. That kind of shit didn't happen over night.

"Look, Loyal, don't try and act like you didn't see this coming. We haven't been happy for a while."

"Really, Ariel? You wasn't saying that shit when I was dicking you down five minutes before it was time for me to leave and catch my flight for Colorado. You seemed pretty fuckin' happy then. Or two weeks ago when we were on a yacht in fuckin' Puerto Rico!" I grimaced.

"Well, I figured I'd give you some one last time before I left you," she shrugged nonchalantly.

I didn't hit women, but I wanted to get up and choke the shit out of this bitch. Not one time had she shown any signs that there were problems in our relationship. Now, all of a sudden, she was unhappy and wanted out? Shorty had the game fucked up if she thought I'd let her skip off that easily. I had upgraded this bitch's whole lifestyle over the time we'd been together. She'd gone from public housing, Ramen noodles and Rainbow, to living lavish, eating steak, shrimp, and lobster, while rocking all of the latest designer fashion. If it wasn't for me, her ass would've still been down bad, living check to check.

Clenching my jaws together, I exhaled heavily through my nostrils. "Aight, bet. You can go, but you leaving this bitch with everything you came with," I told her, standing to my feet.

"E - excuse me?" she blinked expeditiously.

"You heard what the fuck I said. You got a new nigga, right? Well, tell him you need some new shit because anything my paper paid for, stays." I sucked my teeth.

A mean scowl graced Ariel's face as her nostrils flared and her chest heaved up and down. I could tell I'd just crushed her soul. Her ass lived for material shit, so I knew her heart was breaking just thinking about having to leave the shit I'd bought. Good! She'd broke my shit, so she could call it even.

"Fine, Loyal. Since you wanna be petty, FINE! You can have all of this shit. I'm out!" she barked, before snatching her keys from the dresser and brushing past me, heading for the door.

"Ayo, Ariel," I called out after clearing my throat. Making an about-face, she turned and shot me an evil glare. "You may wanna call an Uber or Lyft or some shit. You forgot that truck belongs to me, too." I held my hand out for the keys.

If that bitch was leaving me, she was leaving everything attached to me. Despite how much I loved Ariel, I wasn't no sucka ass nigga.

# Rhymedi

"So how have things been going lately?" my mother asked as we sat at my kitchen table, conversing over lunch.

On Thursdays, when Brittani worked her second job, my mother would come by to check on me and help with the things I needed. This particular Thursday, she'd come a little earlier than usual and brought one of my favorite things to eat— a chicken California sub from Jersey Mike's. The kind gesture made me smile, since it was one of those days where I was down in the dumps, feeling sorry for myself. It was a beautiful day outside, yet, I felt gloomy on the inside. Not to mention it was the first off day I'd had in a while, and instead of being able to go out and enjoy it like a normal person, I was stuck in the house, in a stupid chair.

"Things are okay, I guess," I shrugged indifferently, before taking a bite out of my sandwich.

I really wanted to tell her that I was miserable as fuck and hated life at the moment, but I didn't feel like hearing her preach about how blessed I was to even be alive. I didn't care how true the shit was. It wasn't going to change me being in this fucked up situation, and it damn sure wasn't going to stop the suicidal thoughts I had on the regular.

"You sure about that? Your reply didn't sound too convincing," my mother side eyed me.

Sighing heavily, I rolled my eyes to the top of my head. "Yes, ma, I'm sure, dang. Leave it alone, please," I snapped.

"Dang? Girl, who you think you're snapping at like that? You may be grown, but you ain't damn crazy!" she spat, giving me a stern look. "I'm your mother, Rhymedi! You think I don't know when you're not okay?" she then asked.

Smacking my lips with guilt, I looked up at her with puppy dog eyes. "I know, ma, I apologize. Today is just one of those days. My back and legs have been aching, and I'm just not feeling this whole being in a chair thing. Like, why me? What did I do that was so bad to deserve this?" I pouted, as I fought hard to keep the tears from falling. "I hate it here."

"Rhymedi Patrice Givens!" my mother snapped, addressing me by my full name. She only did that shit when I was doing something wrong, so I knew she was about to get in my ass. "What have I told you about that pitiful shit? Why not you? You're human, just like anyone else. Meaning, it doesn't exempt you from anything. Now, you may not like it, but this is your new normal, and we have to deal with it!"

Batting my eyes, huge teardrops fell as I began to sniffle. I hated when my mother came down so hard on me. Although I knew it was tough love to help me grow thicker skin, it still hurt my feelings. She would always tell me that she wasn't giving me a pity party or allowing me to wallow in my misery, but I wasn't asking for that. All I wanted was for her to understand my feelings, and I knew it would never happen because the shit wasn't happening to her. She could walk just fuckin' fine.

"I know, ma. I know," I sniffled. "It's just so hard adjusting to something like this. I went from being able to do everything on my own to needing assistance with everything. I can't even make a move without this dumb ass chair! The shit is so embarrassing. On top of that, my fiancé left me for a normal girl, and I have no life. I fuckin' hate my life, ma!" I cried, shaking my head in defeat.

Getting up from the chair across from me, my mother walked around the table and took a seat in the one next to me. Pulling me into her embrace, she consoled me until my soul was cleansed. When I was finished, she gently grabbed ahold of my chin and lifted my head until my teary eyes met hers.

"It's okay to cry sometimes, Rhymedi, and it's okay to feel defeated. But what's not okay, is staying there. As I've told you a million times before, this chair doesn't define you. You're still a beautiful, talented, STRONG black woman. I didn't raise you to be weak, Rhym, and I won't start now because you're in that chair. You can still make anything you had planned for your life before becoming paralyzed happen.. It may be a little harder, but you can do it, baby. I believe in you." She ran her fingers through my dreadlocks, soothing me. "And as for Terry's coward ass, fuck him, baby. This was God's way of showing us that he wasn't the man for you, because if he loved you, he'd still be here."

Sniffing, I ran both of my palms down my wet face. "Yeah, I guess you're right," I then murmured.

"Guess? Chile, please. When have I ever given you false information?" she side eyed me, causing me to chuckle.

"Never," I replied honestly.

"I know! Because as your mother, I will never tell you anything I don't know to be facts. And one day, you're going to meet a man who'll worship you and love you beyond that chair," she then told me.

"Okay ma, now you're pushing it," I scoffed, rolling my eyes to the top of her head.

"Okay, whatever you say. But mark my words."

Chuckling, I shook my head in shame. "Whatever, ma. I'm done with this conversation. I just wanna eat my sandwich in peace," I then told her before picking up my sub and taking another bite.

"That's fine, we can change the subject. I have something else I want to talk to you about anyway."

"Oh, really? And what might that be?" I asked, curious as to where she was about to take the conversation next.

"Brittani told me she asked you to go to Calabasas with her for Sp —,"

"Oh, God, ma, not she called you," I huffed, cutting her off before she could even finish her statement. "I don't know why she be calling herself telling on me, like that's going to change my mind." I rolled my eyes in frustration as I made a mental note to curse my cousin out as soon as she brought her ass home.

"Well, wait, Rhym, just hear me out for a minute," my mother pleaded.

"Okaaay, mama, go," I huffed, motioning my hands for her to speak.

"I really think you should go. This would be good for you. I can't remember the last time you've been anywhere. Plus, Calabasas is a beautiful, peaceful place. Your dad and I used to visit almost every summer before you were born. To be honest, it's where you were conceived," she winked before letting out chuckle.

"Okay TMI, ma. I didn't need to know all of that." I turned up my top lip, causing her to fall out laughing.

"Alright, I'm sorry. But on a serious note, you should really give it some thought. I promise, you'll love it," my mother smiled.

Smacking my teeth, I let out a light breath. "I don't know, ma."

"Seriously, Rhym, just think about it. You can either sit in that chair and let life pass you by, or you can embrace your new normal and live your best life. It's all up to you," my mother scoffed, leaving me speechless.

As I sat at the kitchen table with her last statement heavy on my brain, something clicked. And it was at that moment I decided I was going to take my life back.

# Homicide

*Pointers in the Patek and my piece*

*I'm pushin' P*

*Copped new hammers for my P*

*we don't want no peace*

*Got a spot across the spot*

*just for Ps*

*Dropped the dot and then we plottin'*

*xotic Ps*

The sound of Gunna and Future's hit single, Pushin P, blared through the surround sound speakers of my game room as Menace, Havoc, and I stood around, shooting a game of pool. It was something we did when we got together to discuss all the bullshit going wrong in our lives.

"So the bitch just left? No warning, no explanation; just shook the spot?" Menace asked before leaning over the table, striking one of the balls into the right corner pocket.

"Hell yeah," I replied before taking a sip of the 1942 I had occupying my glass. "Shit, if I wouldn't have come home early from Denver, I wouldn't have even caught her sneaky ass. Then the bitch had the nerve to be wearing another nigga's ring," I scoffed, sucking my teeth in frustration.

"Damn, she played you like a goofy, dawg."

"Fuck you mean, like?" Havoc chuckled, intervening. "His ass is a fuckin' goofy. Goofy as fuck for fuckin' with that no good ass, Kardashian wannabe ass bitch."

"Aye bruh, chill the fuck out." I shot him an evil glare.

"Man, what? Truth hurts, huh, nigga? You should have listened to me when I was trying to warn you about the broad, and yo' ass wouldn't be sitting up here looking like a sick ass puppy," he finished before pulling a fat ass pre-rolled Backwood from his ear and sparking it up. "I could smell the hoe in her the first day you brought her goose neck ass around," he then stated, causing Menace to fall out laughing.

"Aw man! Bro, you a damn fool. What hoe smell like?"

"Japanese Cherry Blossom, Cucumber Melon, Champagne Toast, and anything Vanilla. If she wear any of those scents, she a certified hoe!" Havoc replied like the shit was law.

Sucking my teeth, I gave his dumb ass the side eye. "Nigga, shut yo' dumb ass up!" I then told him before snatching the Za from his grasp, taking a long drag.

I loved my little brother, but his ass always had some ignorant ass shit to say — especially when it came to Ariel.

"Fuck you, nigga! You only mad 'cause I'm spitting facts. Ariel big teeth ass stayed wearing all those cheap ass scents. Only bitch I know with a rich ass nigga but still wearing Bath & Body Works. You should've known the bitch wasn't right, bro," Havoc shook his head in disappointment.

"Bro, chill the fuck out, PLEASE. I really ain't in the mood for yo' shit tonight, DAMN!" I killed the rest of the liquor in my glass before passing the blunt to Menace and preparing to take my turn at the table.

I couldn't lie, a nigga was in his chest, and the last thing I wanted to hear was my little brother cracking jokes like he was auditioning for a spot on *ComicView* or some shit. I didn't care how accurate the shit was. Ariel might have been playing on a nigga, but the shit I felt for her was real. Out of all the women I'd been with, she was the first that made a nigga really want to settle down. I guess it was karma for all the bitches I'd done dirty, when they just wanted to build with a nigga.

"Awww, that po' baby heartbroken?" Havoc was still with the shit. "You want me to call mommy so she can whip her titty out for you? Ole cry baby ass boy." He fell out laughing as Menace joined him. These fuck ass niggas were really laughing at my pain.

"I swear, yo' ass a fuckin' fool, bro," Menace stated in between breaths. "I'm just trying to figure out how you know all the names of those damn scents?!"

"'Cause his ass a hoe too!" I answered.

"You fuckin' right. I love the hoes, baby," Havoc patted his chest proudly.

"Ole sick ass," I sucked my teeth.

"Yep. And when I need healing, I'll marry me a doctor — not a Bath & Body Works wearing bitch like you." He busted out laughing again.

"Yeah, aight. Get ya giggle on, fuck boy. You got it." I tilted my head at him before striking the eight ball into the left, middle pocket. "Game, bitch!" I then threw the stick onto the table.

"What, nigga?! Neva!" he looked at the table in disbelief.

"Yeah, nigga! So busy running your fuckin' mouth instead of paying attention to the game. Run me my money, bitch!" I rubbed my fingertips together.

Sucking his teeth, Havoc huffed before digging into the pocket of his denim Amiri jeans. Pulling out a thick ass wad of cash, he peeled off two crisp, blue hundred dollar bills and slapped them in the palm of my hand.

"Here, bitch. A bet is a bet. I want my fuckin' rematch, though. Double or nothing."

"Aight, bet," I chortled, stuffing the money in my pocket.

Looking over at Menace, I cleared my throat. "You too, nigga. Run me my dough."

"What? Nigga, I was just shooting for my homie while he rolled the weed. This wasn't my game," he scoffed.

"Fuck that, nigga. You grin, you in. Now pay up, bitch."

"Man," Menace sucked his teeth. "You shol' right," he nodded, pulling out a stack and peeling off my bread.

"Nice doing business with you," I laughed as he tossed the money onto the table.

"Yeah, whateva, nigga. That's chump change to a boss."

"Aw, yeah? Well, double down with ya boy, then."

"Bet, say no more, bitch!" he tossed another two hundred on the table.

"Man, fuck that. Menace, keep yo' money, bruh. This nigga just mad 'cause we was clowning that Mr. Ed looking hoe of his," Havoc barked. "I already put double up, now rack the fuckin' balls, Keith Sweat," he then told me.

"You gon' keep talking, and I'ma put a hot one in yo' ass!" I picked up the pool stick and pointed it in his direction.

"Yeah, okay. You should've had this same energy with that big head bitch," he stated, passing me the blunt. "Aye, but serious question, though."

"What, bitch?" I shot him an evil glare. I just knew he was about to ask some dumb ass shit.

"Did she at least give you your ring back?"

"You damn right! I made that bitch leave everything I spent my bread on."

Smiling big as fuck, Havoc rested his hand on my shoulder. "Damn, nigga, you ain't as goofy as I thought. I'm proud of you, bro."

"Man, shut yo' dumb ass up and break," I grimaced,

shrugging his hand off of my shoulder.

Laughing his ass off, Havoc leaned over the table and broke the pyramid, striking a couple of stripped balls into the pockets. "But on some real shit, a nigga's thirty-first just a few days away, and I got some shit in the works. The last thing I need is your heart broken ass down in the dumps. I'ma need for you to pull yourself together, bro." He then looked up at me.

"Fuck you mean, pull myself together? Nigga, I'm straight! Did I love Ari, yes. But I ain't losing no fuckin' sleep," I made shit clear.

"Good! 'Cause I need the old Homicide back. My chick coming to visit from St. Louis, and she's bringing a couple of her girls with her to our beach house in Calabasas. From the pictures she sent, they're bad as fuck, so I'm sure one of them can occupy your time for the weekend. At least, that's what I'm hoping."

"Shiiid, if they can't occupy his, they can damn sure occupy mine," Menace added, rubbing his hands together like Birdman.

"I mean, if they as bad as you claim, I'm with it. I'm a free agent now," I smirked.

"See, now that's the type of shit I like to hear," Havoc grinned, dapping me up. "RETURN OF THE MUTHAFUCKIN' MACK! MY BROTHER IS BACK!" his silly ass then yelled.

"I swear, yo' ass a fool! Man, pass me the bottle," I chuckled as he passed over the 1942 bottle, and I proceeded to refill my glass.

Though my mouth was saying one thing, my heart felt the complete opposite. I was sick as fuck that Ariel had walked out on a nigga, but I refused to let these niggas see me sweat. I was going to take advantage of this little Calabasas getaway.

"Girl, I can't believe this nigga done flewed us out on a private jet! And it's huge and nice as fuck too!" our cousin, Alicia, squealed, as we boarded this pretty ass private jet, preparing to take off for California.

As Brittani and Monica picked me up from my chair and carried me to my seat, I still couldn't believe I'd left the comfort of my home. I felt nauseous, and my mind was racing a mile a minute. The brims of my eyes burned from being ready to burst into tears at any second, and it was taking everything in me to not scream out for them to take me back. Yet, I remained cool on the outside because I also wanted to try something different for once.

"Girl, ain't it?! What that nigga do for a living, and do he got a brother? A bitch tryna be down like Brandy!" Monica blurted as she and Brittani sat me down in the soft, peanut butter leather seats. They were comfortable as hell and smelled so good.

Inhaling the scent, I slowly ran my hands up the armrest. When I got to the headrest of the seat next to me, I noticed the initials *TBC* stitched inside of the leather. I began to wonder what it stood for. I didn't know much about this Havoc guy that my cousin was talking to, but whoever the nigga was, it was clear, he was a certified fuckin' boss. Jets weren't cheap and by the looks of this one, he'd paid a pretty damn penny! If not two.

"He owns a few weed farms here and there," my cousin blushed, as she took a seat near me. "And yes, he has an older brother, who happens to be his business partner."

"Oooh, shit! I knew I was gonna find me a man on th —,"

"BUT," Brittani continued, cutting her off. "I believe he has a fiancée," she snickered.

"DAMN! Ain't that some shit?" Monica pouted, flopping down into her seat.

"Haaaaa!" Alicia teased, sticking out her tongue. "Looks like yo' thirsty ass ain't finding shit."

"Fuck you!" Monica flipped her the bird. "Ole big lip, Adele Givens lookin' ass hoe!"

"Yep! All that! But I got a nigga, though!" Alicia shot back.

"Yeah, one that's broke and always cheating on yo' dumb ass! You can have that!"

"I mean, if you wanna fight, bitch, SAY THAT!" Alicia jumped up from her seat, ready to rumble.

"Bitch, what's up?" Monica was about to run at her until Brittani jumped up between them.

"AYE, NO! ENOUGH!" she yelled, grimacing at one to the other. "Now I didn't bring y'all on this trip to act all ghetto and shit! I told y'all before we left to leave whatever beef y'all got back at my house."

"It ain't no beef; that ugly ass hoe just jealous!" Monica spat, rolling her eyes.

"Nah bitch, you the ugly one."

"HEEEY!" I screamed, tired of hearing their asses bicker. "Newsflash, y'all sisters and look just the fuck alike. BOTH y'all asses ugly!"

These bitches had some nerve to be calling one another ugly. They shared the same mama and daddy, yet, they couldn't stand one another. It had been this way since we were little. I never liked going anywhere with them because they stayed embarrassing us, fighting like bitches from the streets. Part of me agreeing to come on this trip was based on them promising to treat one another right. We hadn't even gotten comfortable on the jet, and these hoes were already clowning. I was over it.

"Now please, sit down and shut the fuck up, DAMN! We on this nice ass jet, and y'all wanna act like heathens! If y'all gonna continue this lame ass arguing shit, I'll gladly call my mother and have her pick me up because that's not what I came for," I fussed, pulling out my cell.

The aircraft got so damn quiet, you could hear a pin drop. All eyes were on me as the three of them shared the expressions of scared toddlers. A part of me wanted to burst out laughing, but I needed them to know I meant business. I had been promised the time of my life and so far, these bitches weren't holding up their end of the bargain.

"Oh no, cousin, I'm sorry. Please don't call Aunt Laura; we want you to stay with us." Alicia took the seat next to me and pulled me in for a hug. "See, Monica, look what you did. You've upset my big cousin."

"Me?! Bitch, you the one started it, talking about me not being able to find a man," Monica popped her lips, rolling her eyes.

"Look, who cares who did what?! The point is, y'all grown as fuck and acting like fuckin' kids! On top of that, y'all are family—sisters! Y'all need to get this shit together, or I'll send both of y'all back home in an Uber, because Rhymedi is going to Cali with me!" Brittani snapped. "Now, what y'all wanna do?" she then asked, looking back and forth from Alicia to Monica.

"We wanna go to Cali," Monica mumbled like a scolded toddler.

"And what about you?" Brittani then turned to Alicia.

"We wanna go to California," Alicia mumbled.

"Okay then, act like it and quit acting like fuckin' animals. We ladies and we getting flewed out by a BOSS NIGGA!"

"Eeeeoooowww!" Monica adlibbed, sticking her tongue out, wounding one arm in the air like Cardi B. You right, cousin. I apologize for my behavior," Alicia spoke up. "And I apologize to you too, sis. I shouldn't have said what I said," she then turned to Monica.

"It's all good, boo. I know you love me." She blew Alicia an air kiss.

"Awwww, see now look at that! What's so hard about loving on your sister?"

"Man, Monica know I love her; we just butt heads sometimes. It's just our way of showing our affection. We sisters, we can do that. Bet no other bitch try her, though! I'll stomp a hoe ears together," Alicia scoffed.

"And that's on Mary and that little ugly ass LAMB!" Monica added, causing us to all fall out laughing.

Our snickering came to an abrupt halt when we heard the sound of someone clearing their throat. Looking up, we noticed a beautiful ass foreign bitch, dressed as a flight attendant. As she began to speak, we gave her our undivided attention.

"Good evening, ladies. My name is Blanca, and I will be your flight attendant for the next few hours. If it's not a problem, the captain asks that you all take your seats and prepare for takeoff. We ask that you buckle up and stay seated, until further notice. The ride will be about three hours and forty-five minutes. We also have complimentary beverages and snacks if any of you would like to partake," the woman politely stated.

"Well, thank you, Ms. Blanca, we appreciate the important information," Brittani smiled. "I just have one question."

"Yes ma'am, I'm here to answer any questions you may have."

"Do those complimentary beverages contain alcohol?"

"Yes ma'am," Blanca snickered. "Top shelf."

"Did she just say top shelf?" Alicia's ghetto ass tried whispering to Monica, but we all heard her.

"Yes ma'am, I did." Blanca nodded in confirmation.

"Well, in that case, I'll take a 1942 with a side of lime juice. And I'ma need that before we take off, 'cause I ain't neva been on no plane before, and a bitch is petrified, okay!" Alicia popped her lips.

"Yes ma'am, coming right up," Blanca nodded. "Will the rest of you ladies like anything before takeoff?"

"Yes. I'll take a lemon drop," Brittani spoke up.

"Yeah, I think I want one of those, too," I added.

"Okay, and you, ma'am?" She turned to Monica.

"Y'all got Hennessy?"

"No Ma'am, but we have Louis XIII."

"Ooooh, that's that rich people shit, huh?" Monica asked, causing the woman to chuckle hard as fuck. She was just ghetto by nature.

"Yes ma'am, if that's what you'd like to call it."

"Aw shit, yeah! I want that, give me that. I ain't ever had rich people cognac before," she smiled big as fuck, rubbing her hands together.

"Yes ma'am, coming right up. You beautiful ladies hang tight." She disappeared to go fulfill our requests.

"Oooooh shit, this shit is LIT! I can't believe we're on a jet getting rich bitch services!" Alicia squealed.

"Well believe it, bitch! It's up and fuckin' STUCK! 'Cause when we get to Calabasas, I'm putting this snatch on his ass to make SURE this nigga don't go NOWHERE!" Brittani giggled.

"Bitch, you BETTA! Shit, if I would've known you could meet niggas like this on Instagram, I would've replied to some of these "Hey beautiful" DMs!" Monica smacked her lips, causing us to fall out laughing.

When Blanca came back with our drinks, the girls got seated, and we prepared for takeoff. As I sipped on my lemon drop, I began to think maybe this trip wouldn't be so bad after all.

∞ ∞ ∞

Almost four hours later, we landed in California. As I gazed out of the window of the jet, I spotted a black on black 2022 Escalade EXT with limousine tint, waiting on the strip. There was a sexy, muscular, bald brother standing outside of it, dressed like he was auditioning for a role in *Men in Black*. I assumed he was the driver.

"Awww shit, y'all, LOOK!" I pointed in excitement. "I wonder if he's waiting for us."

"Daaaam! Is that the new Escalade?" Monica squinted.

"Yep!" I giggled.

"Shit, fuck the Escalade! Who is the fine ass nigga standing outside of it?" Alicia added, licking her lips hungrily.

"Here yo' ass go," Brittani snickered. "According to Havoc, his name is Murda, and he'll be driving us to the beach house," she informed us.

"Well, he damn shol' can murder this pussy!" Alicia uttered, causing us all to bust out laughing.

"And wait, did you just say BEACH house?" Monica placed emphasis on the word *beach*.

"Yep, sure did!" Britt nodded with a grin. "I told y'all this trip will be unforgettable," she winked.

"Lord, I think I've died and gone to heaven!" Monica clutched her chest.

"Nope, this reality, baby! Now let's get cousin in this truck! Alicia, you get her chair," Brittani ordered.

As she and Monica carried me to the Escalade, Mr. Murda loaded our bags and my chair into the back. When we were all packed in and ready to go, he cranked up the truck, and we were on our way.

"Good day, beautiful ladies. I'm sure my boy has already informed you of who I am, but in case he didn't, the name's Murda, and I'm your chauffeur for the afternoon. The ride will be about forty-five minutes, so make yourselves comfortable. There's a complimentary bottle of Ace of Spades, along with four champagne glasses back there in the middle console; help yourself. If you need to make a stop or have any questions, press the red button next to the door handle, and I'll let the glass down. In the meantime, you ladies enjoy the ride."

Murda peered through the rearview mirror before licking his thick, pillow soft lips, causing my center to pulsate. Those bitches looked just as good as he did, if not better. I had to turn my head to prevent myself from staring. If you were to look up the word *handsome* in the dictionary, I was sure his picture would be right next to it.

"Well, Mr. Murda, it's nice to meet you. I do have just one question, though," Alicia smacked her lips.

"Yes ma'am, what's that?"

"You single?"

"ALICIA!" we all spat in unison.

"Whaaaat?! I just wanna know!" she shrugged.

Chortling, he smiled, showing his perfect, pearly white teeth. "As a matter of fact, I am," he winked, blowing her a kiss.

Giggling, Alicia began fanning herself. "Oooh boy, you better stop playing with me. I've been known to suck a grape through a straw." She then ran her tongue across her top lip, causing the whole car to erupt in laughter.

"Okay, I'm sorry, Mr. Murda, but y'all can finish this conversation on y'alls own time; we about to pop this bottle," Monica stated, retrieving the Ace of Spades from the console.

"You ain't said shit but a word," he nodded. "I'll get at you before we part ways, lil' baby. Keep that energy," he winked at Alicia before letting up the glass that separated the front from the back.

"Oh, he getting fucked tonight," Alicia giggled once it was all the way up.

"Ole freaky ass! But hey, I ain't mad at you! Live your life; we on vacation!" I shrugged. "Just make sure you wrap it up."

"AND, make that nigga's toes curl!" Monica added.

"PERIOD!" Brittani put the cherry on top as we fell out laughing.

Popping the bottle, she then poured champagne in all of our glasses, and we sipped the rest of the way to the beach house.

The home was breathtakingly beautiful. After getting settled in, Britt pushed me around as we all took a quick detour of the place. She announced that I would be the one to take the master room since I was the one who'd need the most space. With eight bedrooms and six and a half bathrooms, it was located right off of the water. Like, you could literally walk out the backdoor and be on the beach. There was a game room with a huge ass bar, stocked with nothing but the best wines and spirits. The best part of the home was the elevator and the bowling alley. I'd only witnessed this kind of shit in movies, so for it to actually be my reality was mind blowing.

After our tour, we made it to the kitchen, where we found a spread of delicious looking fruit and finger-food platters, along with more bottles of champagne, resting on the spacious marble topped island. In the center was a huge vase of long stem pink roses, an ounce of weed, and a card. Snatching the card, Britt immediately began reading.

"What it do, beautiful? I hope you and your girls enjoyed your flight. Here're a few refreshments and some good bud to help with the jet lag. Murda will be back in a few hours to take you ladies shopping. Spare no expense! It's my birthday, so I want you ladies to look your best. Tonight, we party, so be ready by eleven sharp. Havoc." My cousin was smiling from ear to ear as she finished reading the card. "Oh my God, he's treating us to a shopping spreeee!" she squealed, jumping up and down.

"HELL YEAH! See now, that's what the fuck I'm talking about! This nigga is definitely a keeper; shit just keep getting better and better," Monica stated, stuffing grapes into her mouth.

"Okaaay!" Alicia slapped fives with her sister. "She said this trip would be epic, but damn, I ain't expect celebrity service. Cousin, when you get the chance, you better suck his dick from the back!"

"And lick the gooch too!" Monica added as they both fell out laughing.

"Y'all so damn stupid," Britt chuckled.

Sighing heavily, I smacked my lips. "Well, y'all have fun. Looks like I'll be here alone tonight."

Quickly snapping their necks in my direction, they all gave me a smug look. "Uh uh, fuck you mean? You're going out with us!" Brittani spoke up.

"Uhm, no, I'm not. Y'all know damn well I don't do clubs. Ain't shit changed because we're in a different city," I sucked my teeth and rolled my eyes.

"Who said anything about a club?" Alicia questioned.

"Club, party, get together, whatever. I'm not going! I hate being around crowds. I'm good."

Smacking her lips, Monica pouted like a mad toddler. "Damn, really, cuz?"

"Uh, really," I nodded seriously.

"See, that's not fair. You promised that you would come and live your best life. How you gon' do that sitting up in the house?" Alicia stated.

"I don't know," I shrugged. "But I'll figure it out."

It wasn't that I didn't want to go. I just wanted them to go and have fun without having to worry about me. Tagging along would only put a damper on their fun, and I hated feeling like a burden. But I didn't want to tell them that because they'd only try to convince me otherwise.

"Man, you WACK!" Monica shouted, as Brittani fell out laughing. "And what the fuck you laughing at? This ain't funny."

"Y'all letting her ass upset y'all. I ain't thinking 'bout Rhym's ass. That bitch going wherever the hell I go," Brittani stated, grabbing one of the bottles of champagne.

"Oh, is that right? Says who?" I asked with a raised brow.

"Says me."

***POP!***

Brittani smiled as champagne oozed from the top of the bottle.

"Yeah, that's the one, my nigga. That shit is fly as fuck, my boy!" I assured my little brother as he stood in the full body mirror, dressed in a custom made suit.

We were getting ready for his big birthday bash, and the homie, Vincent Bouchelli, had hooked him the fuck up. He was one of the most requested designers in L.A. He had a waiting list so long, it was impossible to get anything made, unless you were VIP. Let's just say me and my brother were very important niggas. Anytime we needed my guy, he was just a phone call away.

"Vincent muthafuckin' Bouchelli! You don't miss, do you, my boy?" Havoc chuckled, tugging at the collar of the suit jacket.

"Well, I try not to, my friend," V replied in his thick, French accent. "I have to admit, you compliment my work well. Looks good on you, buddy," he patted little bro on the shoulder.

"Ooooh wee," Havoc rubbed his hands together. "The hoes gon' wanna suck a young nigga's dick through my suit pants," he then chuckled hard as fuck.

"Aw shit, here yo' ass go with the clown shit. Nigga, take that shit off so we can be out; we got shit to do," I chortled. "Bouchelli, drape this shit up and give us our ticket so we can take care of you and bounce, before this nigga say anymore dumb shit," I shook my head in shame.

"Hey, what's the problem, buddy? I'm with Havoc. There's absolutely nothing wrong with a little tongue and balls action," he chuckled.

"Exactly, V, tell his ass," Havoc scoffed. "When niggas in a drought, they tend to hate on niggas like you and me." They both fell out laughing as they dapped one another up.

"Aight, you know what? Fuck y'all! I'll be up in the front. Hurry yo' punk ass up, nigga," I grimaced as I headed towards the front of the shop.

"Damn, bitch boy, get out yo' feelings. I was just fuckin' with you!" Havoc yelled out, but I kept walking.

I didn't have time for his bullshit ass shenanigans at the moment. Ever since Ariel had walked out on a nigga, his ass had been cracking jokes. At first, the shit didn't bother me because that was just the type of nigga Havoc was; he was a goofy ass nigga. But as the days went on, the shit was starting to get old. I was trying to get over the shit between Ariel and me, and it was hard to do when he brought her up every chance he got. Shit, I hadn't even told everyone we'd split up.

Taking a seat in one of the chairs near the entrance, I pulled out my phone and proceeded to return a few texts. I had a couple of surprises for my little brother tonight. One being the custom 2022 Rolls-Royce Wraith he'd been wanting. He was going to lose his shit when I had Menace pull up to his party and toss him the key fob. I couldn't wait to see the expression on his face. It had been a long time coming. Just a little over a decade ago, we were just dirty ass poor niggas, hustling out of ounces. Now, we were bosses who owned over ten weed farms. It was only right to ball out on my little nigga for his G-Day.

As I had my head buried into my phone, I heard the bell from the door, alerting that someone had entered. Paying it no mind, I continued doing what I was doing, until I heard a familiar voice.

"Bouchelli, darling, we have arrived."

It was Ariel. She was dressed up like some boujee ass white bitch, with a Chanel scarf tied down her face and big Chanel sunglasses covering her eyes. She cradled a fluffy white dog in one hand and the hand of some cornball looking ass white man in the other. Grimacing, I sucked my teeth before standing to my feet.

"Fuck you doing here, Ariel?" I asked, sizing the dude next to her up and down.

"Uhm, what does it look like? I have an appointment with Bouchelli. He's designing my wedding gown and my fiancé's tuxedo." She looked up at the Napoleon Dynamite looking ass boy and smiled.

I could feel the hair on the back of my neck stand up, as I clenched my jaws together in anger. How dare this bitch walk up in my boy's spot and think he was about to service her and her new nigga. V was supposed to design our wedding shit, until she just up and walked out on my ass. The bitch didn't even know who Bouchelli was until I introduced her to his ass. She had the game fucked up if she thought my boy was participating in her clown ass circus she called a wedding. Not if I had anything to do with it, anyway.

"The hell if he is," I sneered, sucking my teeth. "You may as well raise the fuck up out of here and find you another designer because my boy ain't doing shit for you or yo' Mr. Magoo lookin' ass man," I nodded in her fiancé's direction.

"Now you just hold it a minute, bud —," Ari held her hand up, stopping him.

"I got this, honey, stay calm," she then stated. "This is my ex. He's just a little butt hurt, that's all," she giggled, turning her attention back to me. "You really shouldn't act this way, Loyal; it doesn't look good on you. Just take your loss like a man and move on. You're a boss, remember? I'm sure you'll find someone soon. I mean, of course she won't be me, but you get the picture." She blew me a kiss followed up with a devilish smirk. "Now where is Bouchelli? I don't have long; we do cake tasting after this." She removed the Chanel frames from her face before flipping her hair in arrogance.

Sucking my teeth, I nodded before letting out a light chortle. It was taking everything in me not to haul off and bat the piss out of this broad standing before me, 'cause it damn sure wasn't Ari. The woman standing before me was unfamiliar as fuck. She was speaking to me like I wasn't the nigga who'd snatched her ass out of public housing and introduced her to a better lifestyle. If it wasn't for me, the bitch would've probably still been staying in a two bedroom apartment, with eight other muthafuckas, eating pack noodles. Now she was standing here with this white man and all of a sudden had amnesia.

Just as I was about to give her hoe ass a piece of my mind, my little brother and Bouchelli appeared from the back. With the devilish grin that appeared on Havoc's face when he noticed Ariel, I knew he was about to get started.

"Well, well, well. If it ain't Grim Flawdashian!" he chortled. "Fuck yo' ugly ass doing here?" he sucked his teeth.

"Fuck you, Lawchaun!" she sneered.

Falling out laughing, Havoc slapped his knee. "Sorry, Botox Barbie, but I wouldn't touch yo' ass with a ten-foot pole — even if you weren't my brother's old work," he told her, causing her to scoff in humiliation. "Bouchelli, why her hoe ass here?" my brother then turned and asked V.

"She claim she has an appointment with him," I intervened, answering my brother's question. "He's supposed to be designing their wedding attire," I finished with a slight chuckle.

"Fuck if he is!" Havoc snapped, looking over his shoulder to Bouchelli, then back to Ariel and her new, corny ass man. "You got the game fucked up if you think you can just walk out on my brother, break his fuckin' heart, then walk up in our peoples' spot with this Mr. Rogers from the neighborhood lookin' muthafucka and think he's about to design y'all's wedding shit, when the plan was for him to start you and bro's wedding shit this week," my brother grimaced, shooting daggers straight through Ariel.

"Wait, so you two are no longer together?" Bouchelli asked, looking confused as fuck.

"Hell nah! This ditzy broad walked out on my brother last week and already found her a new man to leech off of."

"You've never been good at minding you own business," Ariel uttered, squinting her eyes at Havoc.

"Yeah, and you weren't good at pretending to love my brother. Ole gold- digging skank."

"Hey, you watch it, buddy!" Her square ass man tried defending her.

"Aye, Waldo, I will knock yo' bitch ass the fuck out! So I advise you stand the fuck down," Havoc barked, immediately shutting him up.

"Chill, bro, it's all good." I lightly tapped my brother's shoulder, signaling for him to cool down. The last thing I needed was him catching a case for breaking this white boy's face.

"Bouchelli, how much I owe you for them wasting your time? 'Cause she damn sure ain't getting your business," I asked, pulling a knot from the pocket of my Purple jeans.

"Don't bother, my friend. You can't put a price on loyalty." He motioned for me to put my money away. "I'm sorry, Ms. Ari, but we can no longer do business together. Please leave my store – quietly," he then told Ariel with a slight grin.

Ferociously biting into her bottom lip, she stared all three of us down. If looks could kill, we would have been body bag ready. I didn't give a fuck, though. Ari should've known when she walked away from me, she'd walk away from anything or anyone attached to me. If she didn't, she was just as dumb as she looked with all of that damn Botox in her face.

"You know what? Fuck you, Loyal! You're just mad because I left your gullible ass!" she spat with venom. "And fuck you too, Bouchelli; you fuckin' yes man! There're better designers in L.A.

any damn way!" she shot.

"Oh yeah? Well, I hope you don't look for them where you found your surgeon," Bouchelli shot, causing me and bro to fall out laughing.

Ariel gasped, clutching her chest at the epic come back. "Let's go, honey, these animals are beneath us," she spat before turning and practically dragging her fiancé out of the store by his hand. As the door slammed, we were still laughing at Bouchelli's last remark.

"Aye, that was a good ass comeback, my boy. I didn't know you had that shit in you," I stated, peeling off half my stack of cash and slamming it onto his check-out counter. "That's for bro's suit, and the rest is for being a real nigga. We'll see you at the party tonight?" I then asked, heading for the door.

"Of course, buddy, I wouldn't miss it for the world."

"My Spanish, nigga!" Havoc nodded as we left the store to go finish handling some more business before his big birthday bash.

# Rhymedi

*Big ass chain 'round my neck*

*so these niggas know I'm rich, and ion need shit but the dick*

*Big ass stack in my purse*

*So these niggas know I'm workin', I'm holding this Glock in my Birkin*

*Niggas better hold that L tryna come for my pen*

*I'm really finna make another M*

*Now tell me how the fuck I'm in the wrong if I don't want the nigga*

*And he still ain't fuckin' with the bitch*

"Megan's Piano" blasted throughout the club as my cousins and I sat in the VIP section, looking pretty as ever. Though I said I didn't want to come, Brittani drug my ass along anyway. She'd bought me a cute ass designer outfit, got my nails, feet, and lashes done, and even beat my face to the Gods above. I had to admit, I was happy. It had been a while since I'd really felt like myself, and I felt beautiful.

"Girl, it's live as fuck in here!" Monica yelled to Brittani over the music, as she snapped her fingers, swaying her hips from side to side. "And I can't believe we're in VIP! Got a bitch feeling all high class and shit. I swear, yo' nigga is a keeper!" She took her champagne glass to the head.

Monica wasn't telling any lies; bitches were feeling like stars. Brittani's man had us dropped off at the club in a stretched Escalade limo, and when we'd arrived, we were escorted to our private section, where bottles were waiting with our names on them. The shit was lit. Britt wasted no time in popping a bottle of Ace of Spades, getting the party started. We were all on our second glass, feeling good.

"So cuz, I ain't trying to be all up in your business or nothing," Alicia smacked her big ass lips together, "but when we gon' meet the nigga? He just cashing out on bitches, and we don't even know what he looks like," she finished, taking a sip of her drink.

"Y'all do know what he looks like. I showed y'all his pictures," Brittani replied.

"I mean, yeah, but how you know that's the real him? He could be catfishing you."

"Bitch, if flying on a private jet, staying in a big ass beach house, getting taken on a fifty-k shopping spree, and sitting in VIP seems like a catfish to you, you're dumber than I thought."

"Thank you, Monica!" Brittani chuckled, shaking her head. "I swear, I worry about this bitch sometimes."

"Nu-uh, don't do that," Alicia scoffed. "Yeah, he might be paid and all, but what if he splurging and buttering you up to prepare you for how ugly he really is? Bet you ain't think about that, did you?"

"What?" Brittani scoffed. "Girl bye, you sound crazy," she giggled, slapping fives with Monica.

"Nah, she actually got a point," I shrugged, chiming in. "What if he's rich and ugly?"

"Thank you, cousin!" Alicia popped her lips and rolled her eyes. "These hoes act like they ain't ever seen *Catfish* before. Now when the nigga pop up lookin' like Bushwick Bill, don't say we ain't try to warn you," she finished before polishing off her glass, grabbing the bottle for a refill.

"Ha! Real cute and funny." Brittani flipped Alicia the bird. "And it would actually give me something to think about if I didn't know any better but because we FaceTime every damn day, multiple times a day, I ain't worried about none of that goofy shit you talking about. Now, you bitches wanna take some shots or nah?" Brittani asked, getting up from the fluffy couch and grabbing the bottle of 1942 that was sitting on ice.

"Hell yeah! You know we down to take some shots." Alicia bent over and started twerking as Monica slapped her ass, hyping her up.

"Well, not me," I spoke up. "Y'all can drink up."

I knew these bitches were about to get fucked up beyond their limits. So, I needed to stay sober enough to be able to take care of myself. A part of me wished I'd followed my first mind and just stayed home. I hated feeling like the party pooper.

"Man, come on, cuz, don't be like that. Take a shot with us," Brittani nudged me in the arm.

"No! You already know how I get when I drink. I've already had two glasses of champagne. I'm buzzed enough."

"Girl, that ain't shit!" Monica smacked her lips. "At least take one shot with your bitches!"

"Right, come on, one won't hurt," Alicia inserted.

"Please?" Brittani pouted, giving me puppy dog eyes.

Sighing heavily, I leaned forward and snatched a shot glass from the table in front of me. "Alright bitches, just ONE!" I rolled my eyes as I held up my pointer finger.

"That's what the fuck I'm talking about! Pour that shit up!" Monica screamed as the beat of Nicki Minaj's "Do We Have a Problem?", dropped throughout the club, and Alicia went crazy.

One shot turned to two, and two turned to three. Before I knew it, I was dancing in my chair with my hands in the air. I felt good as hell. Being confined to a chair had stripped my life away completely, and I couldn't remember the last time I'd genuinely had fun. Tonight was different. I could honestly say I was having a ball.

"YO, YO YO!" Cutting the music and interrupting our groove, the DJ began yelling into the microphone. "THE MAN OF NIGHT HAS ARRIVED! THAT'S RIGHT, THE BIRTHDAY BOY IS FINALLY IN THE BUILDING. SO, WHATEVER THE FUCK YOU DOIN', STOP AND LET'S SHOW MY NIGGA HAVOC SOME LOOOOOVE!"

*Double up, three or four times I ain't tellin' no lies*
*I just run it up, never let a hard time humble us*
*Double up, I ain't tellin' no lies, I just (yeah)*
*I ain't tellin' no lies, I just*

The DJ dropped Nipsey Hussle's "Double Up" as black and gold balloons and confetti dropped from the ceiling. Everyone's attention was focused on the entrance as two fine ass niggas dressed in all black tailored suits entered the room. The crowd moved aside and made a pathway as the one with the low-cut fade, f1exed and posed for pictures. From the pics my cousin had shown and the way he was acting, I immediately knew it was Havoc. I assumed the sexy ass dude accompanying him, was his brother; they favored.

After giving many daps and hugs, the two made their way over to our section. Excited as hell to finally see her boo, Brittani met him at the rope, throwing her arms around his neck. Spinning her around in a circle, they shared a nice long lip lock before he planted her back on her feet. I could see him introducing her to his brother. After the two shook hands, Brittani walked back over to us with them both in tow.

"Baby, these are my cousins." B was blushing hard as fuck as she held onto Havoc's hand. It was so cute. "That's Alicia," she began pointing, "Monica, and this is the beauty of us all, Rhymedi." She smiled even harder when she got to my name. "Ladies, this is Havoc, the man behind this amazing vacation," she finally finished.

"Okaaay! And he ain't a CATFISH!" Monica put emphasis on *catfish* as she side eyed her sister. "It's nice to meet you, Havoc."

She then stuck her hand out for a shake.

Letting out a light chortle, he placed his hand into hers. "Likewise, miss lady."

"We've heard so much about you."

"All good, I hope."

"Of course."

"Aw okay, cool." He tugged at his suit collar. "Y'all had a nigga nervous, talking about catfishes and shit," he chuckled.

Smacking her lips, Brittani rolled her eyes to the top of her head. "Don't pay they asses no mind, baby. They just be talking."

"Right, we just like to talk a lil' shit. But it's nice to finally put a face to the name my cousin has been spending all her time blabbing about," Alicia smiled, shaking his hand.

As they were busy introducing themselves to Britt's new boo, I had my eyes locked on his fine ass brother. Tall with the skin color of caramel, his pretty ass hair was neatly styled in cornrows going straight back, draping past his shoulder blades. His mustache was neatly trimmed and complemented the four-inch beard that was just as pretty and full as his hair. The diamonds that graced his neck and wrist danced off the florescent lights, making him look even more appealing. This man was the epitome of gorgeous. I didn't know if it was the liquor or him, but the atmosphere had immediately become toasty, and I began to sweat.

"Rhym!" Brittani was snapping her fingers in front of my face. "Rhymedi!"

"Huh? What?" I finally snapped out of the trance I was in.

"Girl, you good?"

"Yeah, I'm fine," I nervously ran my fingers through my locs. "Why you ask that?"

"Because we've been trying to get your attention, and your

ass just zoned out," Britt snickered, shaking her head.

"Nah, I had just – I mean, I was just…"

"Checking my brother's fly," Havoc chuckled, causing a flush of embarrassment to run through me. "Yeah, I peeped," he let it be known.

"I totally wasn't," I lowered my head in shame.

"It's all good, ma, ain't shit wrong with it. You just like what you see," he shrugged. "Ayo, big bro," he then reached and tapped his fine ass brother's shoulder, causing him to turn around. "You got a secret admirer over here," he nodded in my direction. I immediately became nauseous.

Cracking a million dollar smile, he stroked his beard and walked over to us. "Aw, yeah? Good evening, ladies," he winked simultaneously, licking his supple lips. I could feel my heart begin to palpitate as I envisioned those pretty muthafuckas kissing all over my body.

"Ladies, this is my big brother, Homicide. Bro, this my girl's people. That's Monica, Alicia, and last but not least, the one who couldn't seem to keep her eyes off of you, Rhymedi."

"It's nice to meet you all," Homicide stated, but was only looking at me. The gaze he gave made me feel like a childish schoolgirl who was crushing on her first boy.

Reaching out, Homicide instantly sent chills down my spine as he took my hand into his. He caressed my palm before pulling it up to his lips, kissing the back of it – all while keeping eye contact. "Rhymedi," he recited my name sexily. "A beautiful name for a beyond beautiful woman," he then complimented.

"Thank you," I giggled, batting my eyes bashfully.

"You mind if I sit down with you and have a drink or two?"

Slowly shrugging, I looked from Brittani, to Monica, then Alicia; who were all standing around me, cheesing like Cheshire fucking cats. I was so in disbelief that he was showing interest in me, I honestly didn't know how to respond. I hadn't had any interactions with a man since Terry, and that was about a year ago. I wasn't even sure if I remembered how to entertain one.

"What's wrong, baby? Cat got your tongue now?" Homicide chuckled, still holding on to my hand. "I promise, I don't bite. I mean, unless you want me to." He bit down into his bottom lip, hungrily devouring me with his eyes.

"Whew, chile." Monica took a shot before placing the glass down onto the table. "I think that's our cue to go dance. Sis, you want to go dance with me?"

"Yeah sis, let's," Alicia agreed as they headed for the dance floor.

"I think we should cut a rug too, boo, what you think?" Havoc then looked at Britt.

"I think so too," she giggled, looking over to me.

"Oh wow, you whores real cute!" I gave her the side eye.

"Not as cute as you, boo," she winked. "Have fun." She and her boo proceeded to walk off. "Homicide, take care of my cousin. I'd hate to have to kick your ass about my baby," she then threw over her shoulder.

"Trust me, she's in good hands," he chuckled before taking a seat on the sofa directly next to my chair.

Smiling on the outside, inside, I was a nervous wreck. I could kill my cousins for leaving me alone. Though I was excited to be in the presence of this gorgeous ass man, when I felt the wheels of my chair, I realized he was way out of my league.

*Rhymedi*

I sat up in the VIP area, bobbing my head to the beat of "Rodeo" by City Girls as I watched Monica and Alicia fuck the dance floor up. They were having the time of their lives, hosting a twerk off as the people around them hyped them up – some of them even recording. The brims of my eyes burned as I fought back the tears. I hated that I couldn't get out there with them and have fun too. This was exactly why I didn't like going anywhere. I loved my cousins to death, but I envied them for being able to live their best lives while I was stuck in this dumb ass chair.

It had been a little over ten minutes since Homicide and I had been left alone, and neither of us had yet to say a word. To be honest, I didn't know what to say. I was curious as to what a man as fine and successful as he, saw in a hopeless girl like me, but of course, I was too terrified to ask. I knew he wasn't some sick fuck who had fetishes for girls with disabilities, and he couldn't have possibly felt sorry for me because he didn't know me. Whatever it was had my mind racing and my heart beating a mile a minute.

"Are you always this quiet?" he finally asked, breaking the ice.

"I mean, it depends," I shrugged. "Right now, I don't have anything to talk about."

Chuckling, his sexy ass smiled and stroked that beautiful ass beard, yet again. I guess that was his signature move. "I guess you have a point," he then licked his lips. "Let me give you something to talk about then." He rubbed his hands together.

"Is this your first time visiting California?" Homicide then inquired, engaging a conversation.

"Actually, it is. How'd you know?" I asked with a slight snicker.

"I didn't. I just figured I'd ask," he chuckled. "How are you enjoying your vacation so far?"

"To be honest, I'm having a great time. Everything is so nice, especially the house."

"Yeah, I figured you ladies would love that spot. It's funny because when lil' bro and I first purchased that property, it was a mess. It took a shit load of time and money to get it where it is today; but I don't regret it because it's one of our most lucrative properties. The people love it."

"Oh, wow! That's what's up. It's definitely a beautiful place. So quiet and serene."

"Yeah, you're right about that. It's actually one of my favorite places to visit. I like to walk the beach at sundown. One of the best feelings ever." He stared off in space as if he was actually there in his mind.

As he stared off, I stared at him. Fuck, this man was fine as hell! It had been a while since I'd been in the presence of a man so attractive, and the liquor I'd consumed mixed with twelve months of celibacy had my imagination running wild. I envisioned myself straddled across his lap, sucking on his bottom lip as I ran my fingertips through the parts of his cornrows. My lady parts tingled as I saw him gripping my ass with both palms.

"So, what's your favorite part?" Homicide asked in the midst of my dirty thoughts. I was so busy fucking him in my mind, I'd completely forgotten what the hell we were talking about.

"Uhm, what do you mean?" I asked a bit embarrassed.

"Of the house," he chortled. "What's your favorite part of it?" he clarified his question.

"Oh yeah, that," I snickered. "Uhm, I would have to say it

would be between the bowling alley and the master bedroom; I can't choose. I love the bowling alley simply because I've never, in my life, seen one in a home. And I love the master bedroom because of the view and accessway to the beach. I think that shit is so dope," I smiled, just thinking about it.

"Okay, okay," he smiled, stroking that beard again. "So, have you had a chance to visit the beach yet?" he then asked, making me feel awkward.

"Uhm, nah. I haven't," I replied dryly, hoping he would notice the shift in my attitude and move on to another topic.

"What?! How you staying in a beach house and haven't been to the beach? That's crazy!"

Scoffing, I sucked my teeth in aggravation. "Yeah well, I don't think THESE will make it through some fuckin' sand." I placed emphasis on the word *these* as I pointed to the wheels of my chair. "Therefore, I don't think the beach would be a great idea." I gave a fake ass crooked smile. "Got any other clever suggestions?" I then asked sarcastically.

The smile that was occupying his face quickly disappeared. Clearing his throat, he tugged at his suit tie. "Uhm, I – I sincerely apologize. I didn't even realize you were in a wheelchair," he then stated, making me feel even worse.

Scoffing, I shook my head in shame. "Real cute," I spat. "Look, I don't know what games you're trying to play, but whatever they are, I don't want to play them."

"Games?! Baby, I'm a grown ass man; I don't play games."

"Well clearly, you're on something. Because if you couldn't see that I'm in a wheelchair, you're either blind or –,"

"Or maybe you're so fucking beautiful, I just simply looked right past it," he shrugged nonchalantly.

"Wait, what?" I asked, snapping my neck in his direction.

"You heard me," he licked his lips. "I said, you're just so

fucking beautiful, I looked past the chair. But now that you've brought it to my attention, I see it, and I still don't give a fuck. That chair doesn't have shit to do with who you are as a person. I'm here to get to know Rhymedi, and that's what I'm gonna continue to do," he sucked his teeth. "Now, where were we?"

Speechless, I batted my eyes repeatedly, astonished by his reaction. I would've been lying if I'd said that shit didn't turn me the fuck on. Any other man would've run from my ass, but not Homicide. Me being in a wheelchair didn't move him one bit. It was at that moment, I realized I was dealing with a real nigga.

"Uhm –," I cleared my throat. "About that drink," I giggled.

"Oh now you want a drink?" he chuckled with a raised brow.

"Yes, please," I replied bashfully.

"I got you," he winked, flashing that perfect smile.

Scooting to the edge of the sofa, Homicide grabbed one of the cups from the VIP setup and scooped a few ice cubes into it. He then filled it halfway with 1942 and topped it off with some Ace of Spades. Placing a straw into the concoction, he handed it over to me.

"Wait, Don Julio and Ace of Spades mixed together? I don't know about this," I gave him the side eye.

"Shit fire, trust me. You'll never go back to drinking that shit straight."

"I'm scared," I snickered. "They're both already strong separately, so mixing the two together might be deadly."

"Really, shorty?" Homicide smacked his teeth followed by a light chuckle. "I wouldn't give you shit that would hurt you. I drink the shit all the time. Now come on, just try it. If you don't like it, we'll go with something else."

"Okay, okay; I'll give it a try."

Sighing heavily, I reluctantly placed the straw to my lips and took a sip. Surprisingly, the shit was good as hell. It was smooth, and the slight sweetness of the champagne took away the strong bite of the tequila. It was safe to say, I liked it.

"Mmm, not bad," I nodded in approval.

"See, told you. That's that shit," he chuckled before pouring himself a cup. "But be careful, can't lush it. Your ass will be somewhere slumped," he then warned me.

"Oooh wee! Let me find out you're trying to take advantage of me," I giggled before taking another sip.

"Only if you want me to," he winked, causing me to blush.

Homicide was laying the charm down heavy, and I was eating that shit up like candy. He had my nose wide the fuck open, and I hadn't even been in his presence a full hour. I was interested, and I wanted to know more about him. A part of me wished we could escape the club scene and go to a more intimate atmosphere.

Interrupting my thoughts, Homicide's phone began to go off. He reached into the inside pocket of his suit jacket and pulled it out. Grimacing at the screen, he smacked his teeth before ignoring the call and tossing the phone onto the table. Seconds later, it began to go off again. Letting curiosity get the best of me, I glanced over at the screen. When I noticed the image of a pretty foreign chick, along with the name *Ari* flashing across the screen, I immediately began to feel a way. I could tell by the change in his demeanor and the way he kept sending her to voicemail, she held some sort of substance in his life. Only a woman who held some type of significance in a man's heart could control his feelings like a light switch.

Looking around the club, I proceeded to look for one of my cousins. I had to pee. Plus, I no longer wanted to be alone with Mr. Homicide. Judging from the back to back calls from this Ari chick, it was clear he had some shit going on at home. She'd called seven times within two minutes, so I also assumed the situation was toxic. I didn't like drama, nor was I trying to be someone's rebound or one night stand.

After scanning the room and not seeing either one of my cousins, I proceeded to look around for the restroom. Spotting it, I was relieved when I realized I could get to it on my own. Without thinking twice, I released the brake on my chair and was about to take off when Homicide stopped me.

"Whoa, wait. Where you going, Shorty?" he asked, scooting to the edge of the sofa and placing his drink down.

"I'm going to the restroom, if that's okay with you," I spat.

"Should I go get one of your girls?" he asked with a concerned expression.

"Uhm no, I'm fine."

"You sure? I mean, I can go with you and stand outside of the bathroom if you'd like."

"No, I just said I'll be fine. Now please just – answer your phone or something," I rolled off before he could say anything else.

As I wheeled myself to the bathroom, I prayed my cousins were in there. God must've been busy answering someone else's cry because when I made it inside, there wasn't a person in sight. Thankful that it was at least empty, I rolled to the handicap stall, pulling the door closed behind me. *Shit!* I cursed underneath when I realized the lock was broken.

Sighing heavily, I made my way to the toilet and proceeded to lay toilet paper around the seat. I figured I'd make it quick since it felt as if my bladder would explode, and I really had no other options. Lifting my dress, I pulled my panties down to my knees. I then used my upper body strength to quickly transfer myself from my chair to the commode. I could hear the angels in heaven singing as I threw my head back in exhilaration, releasing the fluids from my bladder. For a moment, I thought I would piss in my chair.

Finishing up, I wiped and flushed. I then scooted to the edge of the seat to prepare to transfer myself back over to my chair. Placing one hand on the railing of the stall and the other on the arm of my chair, I again lifted myself and proceeded to transfer over. I was just inches away from the seat when the chair rolled back, throwing me onto the bathroom tile.

"Fuck!" I swore as I watched my chair push the unlocked door open and roll out of the stall.

Pissed at myself, I began to punch myself in the legs with all my might. "Stupid! Just fucking stupid, Rhymedi!" I cursed myself as tears welled up in my eyes.

Moving too damn fast, I'd forgotten to place the fucking brake on. Now I was stuck on this cold, hard ass floor with my panties around my knees and no one to help.

# Homicide

I watched Rhymedi all the way up until she disappeared off into the ladies' room. Though I had an eerie feeling about her going alone, I pushed it to the back of my mind. I could tell she was already a little timid being in my presence, and the last thing I wanted to do was push the issue and make her even more uncomfortable. So since she said she was good on her own, I was going to take her word for it and just wait patiently for her to get back.

I didn't know what it was about Rhymedi, but the moment I'd looked into her eyes, she'd lured a nigga in. Coming up, my mother would always say that the eyes were the key to the soul, and when I looked in Rhymedi's eyes, it was as if her soul was speaking to me. Not to mention, she was breathtakingly beautiful. She put on this hard, feisty exterior but underneath it all, I could tell she was fragile and needed to be handled with care. I wasn't sure what she'd been through that had her so guarded, but I was hoping she'd let me in enough to find out.

Breaking me out of my thoughts, my phone began to go off again. I looked down at the screen and noticed it was Ariel's ass calling back for the twentieth time. I didn't have the slightest clue as to what she could've been calling about, and to be honest, I didn't give a fuck. She'd chosen her fate the day she'd walked out on a nigga. Therefore, there wasn't shit else to talk about. Plus, she seemed perfectly happy with her new Jerry Springer looking ass fiancé when we'd run into each other at Bouchelli's.

For years, my brother tried warning me that Ariel didn't love me and was only sticking around for a come up. In the back of my mind, I knew the shit was true, but I stuck around, hoping that one day she would grow to love me as much as I did her. Clearly, that day never came. I wanted to be angry, but honestly, I couldn't. Shit, I looked at it as karma for all the women who loved me and I'd done dirty.

When I heard my phone ringing again, I was about to pick up and start cursing, until I noticed my housekeeper, Esmerelda's, name flashing across the screen. She rarely called when I was away, so I knew shit had to be important. Quickly weaving through the club full of people, making my way to the nearest exit, I answered the phone with one hand while using the other to cover my ear and block out the noise.

"Hey, Esmerelda, everything alright?" I got straight to the point as I walked through the threshold of the door, stepping outside.

"No, no! Mr. Taylor, she's here and she's acting like a maniac! Screaming about pearls! Me no have pearls. I have no clue what she's even talking about!" Esmerelda replied, frantic as hell in her thick, Spanish accent.

"Wait, slow down, Esmerelda. Who are you talking about?" I asked, trying to understand what was going on.

"Ms. Harris! She's here and she's crazy!"

***Ding, Dong! Ding, Dong! Ding, Dong!***

I could hear the sound of my doorbell ringing over and over, followed by banging and unintelligible screaming.

"Stop ringing the damn bell and go away! I told you, Mr. Taylor is not home!" Esmerelda yelled. "Mr. Taylor, please come home, quickly," she then begged, sounding scared for her life.

"Esmerelda, I can't come home; I'm in Calabasas for the weekend," I sighed heavily. "But listen to me. I want you to calm down and just walk away from the door. I'm about to call Ariel and see what the fuck her problem is. If you still hear her out there five minutes from now, I want you to sick Georgia on her," I ordered, referring to my American Bulldog that Ariel was terrified as fuck of.

"Okay, okay. Please hurry, Mr. Taylor. My nerves are terrible. I don't like mess!" Esmerelda cried.

"Esmerelda, trust me; I got you. Just walk away. Go down to the bar and have a drink or something. Whatever you like," I told her, hoping it would calm her nerves.

"Thank you, thank you, Mr. Taylor," she replied gratefully.

"You're welcome. Talk to you soon," I told her before ending the call.

Quickly scrolling to Ariel's contact, I called her nutty ass up. It didn't even ring good before she answered my call.

"Ariel, what the fuck are you doing at my crib?" I cursed through gritted teeth.

There were more than a few people standing outside of the club, and the last thing I needed was for them to be in my business. I was a private person, and I hated to be the center of attention.

"I want my pearls, Loyal! Now tell the illiterate, non English speaking ass whore to open up!" Ariel screamed into the phone, causing me to clench my jaws in anger.

"Ari, what the fuck are you talking about? What pearls?"

"The pearls in the jewelry box we shared. Don't play dumb; you know exactly what pearls I'm referring to. Just give them to me, and I'll be on my way. Our jet leaves for Dubai in the morning, and I need them for my wedding day," she explained as if I gave a fuck.

Rubbing the back of my neck, I began to think of just what pearls this crazy broad was talking about. When it finally dawned on me, I began to laugh my ass off.

"Wait, hold up. I know you aren't talking about those pearls my grandmother gave you to wear for our wedding," I asked, making sure I wasn't mistaken.

"As a matter of fact, I am," she replied confidently.

Letting out a faint chuckle, I sucked my teeth in annoyance. "Bitch, you must me out your rabbit ass mind," I then snapped.

"Excuse me?!"

"Yeah, excuse the fuck out of you. I don't now what type of drugs yo' dumb ass smoking, but you gotta be on something strong as fuck to think you're getting the pearls MY grandmother gave you to get married to some other nigga!" I seethed.

"Oh God, here you are being bitter again. Just let it go, Loyal! I'm not marrying you! Besides, she gave the pearls to me. I should be able to do whatever the hell I want with them."

"Bitch, get the fuck off my phone and get the fuck away from my doorstep. You want to get married in some pearls, tell your new man to buy you some. Silly ass hoe," I barked before ending the call.

Going back to Esmerelda's contact, I hit the message icon and shot her a text telling her to let Georgia out. I had never been the type to disrespect a woman, but Ariel had me fucked up. Cleary, she was taking my kindness for weakness, and I didn't like that shit at all. **What type of sucker ass nigga did she think I was to feel that I was going to let her** come back to get the pearls my granny had given her, so she could wear them to exchange vows with any other man. Those pearls had been in the family for generations, and it was going to stay that way. I was keeping them for a woman who truly deserved them.

Slipping my phone into the inside pocket of my suit jacket, I made my way back inside the club. When I approached the VIP section and noticed Rhymedi hadn't gotten back from the ladies' room, I began to worry. I knew Shorty needed a little more time than most to handle her business, but it had been a minute since she'd been in that bitch. Scanning the room for her people so that I could have them go and see about her, that plan fell short when I didn't spot either one of them. Hell, I didn't even see my brother in the building.

Deciding to not waste any more time trying to figure out where they were, I figured I'd go and see about Shorty myself. I had this weird feeling in my gut, and something was telling me something wasn't right. Upon approaching the ladies' room, I opened the door and stuck my head in without thinking twice. When I noticed Rhymedi's wheelchair in the middle of the bathroom floor, my heart dropped to the pit of my stomach.

"Yo shorty, it's Homicide. You alright in there?!" I yelled, before swallowing the lump in my throat.

Hearing the sound of whimpers coming from the back stall, I immediately sprang into protection mode. I barged into the restroom, heading straight for the handicap stall – where I found Rhymedi on the floor soaked in her tears. Kneeling down, I immediately began to help her get herself together. As I was pulling up her panties, Shorty began to sob harder. I could tell it was due to her being embarrassed.

"Shhh, it's alright, Shorty. You good, I got you," I assured her as I wrapped her arms around my neck for support as I pulled her dress down. When she was all good, I then carried her to her chair and gently sat her in it.

"Noooo, no, it's not okay. I want to go home." Rhymedi sobbed even harder. "Oh my God, I'm so ashamed." She shook her head from side to side.

"Look Shorty, you ain't got shit to be ashamed about; shit happens. Now let me see your hands so we can wash 'em."

Still sobbing uncontrollably, she reached her hands underneath the spout of the sink. Turning on the water, I pumped some soap into her hands and helped her wash them. When she was finished, I grabbed a few paper towels and passed them over so she could dry them. After taking them and drying her tears, I then tossed them into the trash.

"No, I don't want to go back out there. Please take me back to the house," Rhymedi sniffled as I proceeded to wheel her towards the door.

"Aight, but I still need to go find your people to let them know we're leaving."

"No, please! I don't want to ruin anyone's fun being worried about me. You can call them once we make it to the house," she peered up at me with pleading eyes. "Please."

Sighing heavily, I ran my hand down my face in defeat. "Aight Shorty, I got you," I then agreed. "Yo' cousin gon' kick my ass!" I then uttered, pushing her out of the bathroom and to the nearest exit.

Once out front, I told valet to bring my whip around. When they did, I placed Rhymedi in the front seat before folding her chair up and putting it in the trunk. Hopping into the driver's seat, I took off, in route of the beach house. The ride was quiet, minus shorty sobbing here and there. I wanted to spark up a conversation, but I knew she wasn't in the mood to talk. Deciding to leave well enough alone, I turned up the music and let Rod Wave talk to us.

Turning a twenty-minute drive into fifteen, I pulled up at the crib. I got out and grabbed the chair before getting Rhymedi out and taking her in.

"Which room you in, Shorty?" I asked, prepared to get her settled in.

"The master, but you can just leave me here; I'll be fine," she stated as we were stationed in the middle of the foyer.

"You sure? I mean, I have no problem helping you get comfortable. You know, since your people aren't here yet," I shrugged, assuring her that it wasn't shit for me to help her.

"No really, you've done enough. I just want to be left alone now."

"Aight, well I'll call my brother and tell him to let your people know you're here," I told her before turning to leave.

"Uhm, Homicide," Rhymedi then called out to me as I opened the door.

"What's up, Shorty?" I turned back to face her.

"Thank you." She gave a faint smile as tears slowly rolled down her cheeks.

"Don't mention it; it's all good."

Walking over to her, I then placed a kiss onto her forehead. "Good night, Shorty."

I left, closing the door behind me. Hopping in my ride, I drove to my hotel room with Rhymedi on my mind.

I sat on the balcony of the room I was staying in, looking out at the beautiful blue water. It was so peaceful and serene. With the night I'd had, this moment was well needed. I was so pissed at my cousins for leaving me all alone; I hadn't said a word to either one of their asses. To be honest, I was just ready to go the hell home. I was over all of this spring break bullshit.

Thinking about Homicide made my heart smile. Though he was the best thing that had happened on this trip thus far, I didn't want to see him again. I was ashamed to. We had only known one another a few hours, and I'd shown my ass — literally. It was embarrassing as hell for him to have to see me that way. How was I supposed to face him after an encounter like that? I couldn't. It wasn't normal for a man to have to care for a woman they way he had, on our first encounter. I felt awful.

Breaking me from my thoughts, I heard a knock at the bedroom door. I turned my head around and noticed Brittani entering with a plate and cup occupying her hands. Rolling my eyes, I sucked my teeth and turned back to the water.

"Hey, I brought you some lunch," she stated softly, extending her arms to hand the dishes over to me.

"Nah, I'm good. I ain't hungry," I declined, eyes glued to the scenery before me. I didn't want shit from her.

"Really, Rhym? Come on now, you gotta eat."

"I said, I'm not hungry. Now please, leave me alone," I asked politely.

Smacking her lips, Britt let out a heavy breath. "Man, how long you plan to be mad for? We've apologized several times about last night. What more you want us to do? Kiss your feet?" she then asked remorsefully.

"Yeah, you guys apologized, but it still doesn't change what happened. At the end of the day, y'all shouldn't have fuckin' left me alone!" I barked.

"We thought you were good. Homicide seemed like a great guy, and he was feeling you, so I gave you your privacy."

"He's definitely a great guy. Shit, if it wasn't for him, I'd still be on the bathroom floor of that fuckin' club! Then, to find out y'all were nowhere to be found because you were in the parking lot smoking WEED! I feel so betrayed," I seethed, shooting her an evil glare.

Brittani's eyes watered as she gave the look of a sad puppy. "That's not fair, Rhymedi. You know I would never intentionally just turn my back on you. You're my baby cousin; I love the fuck out of you. We just got a little too tipsy and carried away."

"And that's exactly why I didn't want to go in the first place. You know how you hoes get in the clubs back home, so you knew how y'all were going to get down out here. Therefore, you should've left me here. But NO, you bitches just had to BEG me to come, only to leave my ass to make a fool of myself," I grimaced, rolling my eyes at her.

"Rhym, it wasn't sup –,"

"Honestly Brittani, whatever you're about to say, I couldn't care less. Just please, leave me be." I focused my attention back towards the water.

"Alright, fine," she scoffed, shaking her head. "Your food will be in here on the nightstand for whenever you're ready. Havoc and Homicide are coming over with a few of their friends, and we're going to have a barbecue and beach day," she then finished.

"Well, good for y'all. Hope you have fun," I uttered, still

facing the water.

"Whatever," Brittani sucked her teeth. "I'm out."

"Bye," I looked back at her, turning up my nose. I'd been asking her to leave since her ass had walked in. She was the one acting as if she couldn't understand English.

Storming out, Brittani slammed the door behind her. I could hear her saying something to Monica and Alicia, but I couldn't make out exactly what it was. At that point, I honestly didn't give a fuck. They could talk all the shit they wanted to. I still wasn't fucking with their asses. Pulling my phone out, I decided to call up my mother. I missed her, and I just needed to hear her voice for comfort. Thankfully, she was available.

"Hey, my beautiful daughter!" She picked up on the first ring, excited to hear from me.

"Hey ma, what you up to?"

"Oh nothing, just putting some dinner on for your daddy so he can have something to eat when he gets home."

"Dinner? This early?" I asked, pulling the phone from my ear, looking at the screen to see that it was just two-thirty in the afternoon.

"Well, it isn't early here, Rhymedi. You guys are two hours ahead where you are, remember? It's thirty minutes 'til five here," she reminded me.

"Aw yeah, you're right. I keep forgetting about the difference in time," I replied with a slight snicker.

"So, how are you today?" she asked, shifting the subject. "How's the west coast treating you?"

Letting out a light sigh, I smacked my lips. "It's cool, I guess."

"Uh oh, I know that tone. What's the matter, baby? You're not having a good time?" my mother asked, voice laced with concern.

"I mean, I was until –," I paused, letting out another sigh.

"What, baby? Talk to ya mama."

Needing to vent, I went ahead and told her everything that had gone down the previous night. By the time I was done, I had a face full of tears. I didn't know what it was that made me so emotional when I talked to my mother, but I turned into a big ass baby every time.

"Awwww, Rhymedi, baby, don't cry. I know you're probably a little ashamed, and your feelings are hurt, but it's okay. You know for a fact Brittani would never intentionally leave you if she didn't feel you were alright. Now as far as Monica and Alicia," my mother scoffed. "I love my nieces to death, but they can barely care for their own damn selves. Just like their mother, just as ratchet and irresponsible as they wanna be," she giggled. "But Brittani, you two have always been more like sisters rather than cousins, Rhymedi."

"I know, ma," I smacked my lips. "That's why I can't understand how she could leave me hanging the way she did. She knows more than anyone how I feel about being in this chair," I uttered.

"And that's exactly how I know she didn't do it on purpose," my mother stated in her favorite niece's defense. "Let me ask you something. And I want you to be one hundred percent honest."

"Aren't I always honest with you?"

"Since you've been in that chair, how many times has your cousin not been there for you?" she asked, causing me to immediately feel guilty.

"Just this once," I mumbled.

"Exactly, and you want to throw her away for just ONE mistake?" my mother asked, making her point valid.

Sighing heavily, the tears began to flow again. "I don't want to throw her away bu –,"

"There is no but, Rhymedi," my mother cut me off. "Next to

me and your father, Brittani has been the one there for you. She even quit her job and left her apartment to move in and care…for you! You need to really think about this situation and cut her some slack. You hear me?" she finished, putting me in my place.

"Yes ma'am," I sniffled.

Even though I was still a bit upset, I had to admit, my mother was right. Brittani had been here with me through it all and never once complained. She'd put her life aside to make sure that I could have one. If that wasn't love, I didn't know what was.

At that moment, I realized my anger wasn't with my cousin. It was with the universe. I couldn't understand why God had chosen me to go through such fucked up circumstances. I was a good ass person and had done nothing to deserve what I was going through. That alone made me bitter as fuck.

# Homicide

"Bruh, last night don't owe me a bitch ass thang! I had the time of my life! There was ass EVERYWHERE!" Havoc laughed before taking a pull from the Backwood full of Obama Runtz we were smoking on.

He, Menace, the homeboy Maniac, and I were on our way to the beach house to kick it with the ladies. We had two big ass coolers filled with food and liquor – we planned on 'cueing and having a little beach day. The girls were only in town for two more days, so we had to make sure we showed them a good time.

"Ass EVERYWHERE!" Menace co-signed. "Too bad you had your bitch in the building and couldn't partake in the festivities."

"Shit, so what?! A nigga was still looking," Havoc chuckled, passing the blunt back to Maniac. "I ain't tripping on that shit anyway. My bitch will give the baddest bitch a run for her money," he sucked his teeth.

"You ain't lyin'. That hoe finer than a muthafucka! Where you meet her at? She got a sister?" Maniac asked, coughing from the weed smoke.

"Aye nigga, watch yo' mouth. Don't be calling my bitch no hoe!"

"But you just called her a bitch," Maniac sucked his teeth. "Fuck on, pussy."

"Nigga, so the fuck what! A bitch and a hoe is two different things. A hoe is worse than a bitch. Now put some respect on my bitch name and don't be calling her no hoe."

"Man, what the fuck ever," Maniac chuckled. "Well, do the BITCH got a sister?" He then asked, placing emphasis on the word *bitch.*

"That's more like it," Havoc stated, causing us all to fall out laughing.

"Man, this nigga is retarded than a muthafucka, boy!" Menace was laughing so hard, he started choking.

"I don't even know why y'all entertain this fool," I shook my head, chuckling.

"Fuck y'all – I'm real," Havoc chortled. "But on some one hunnit shit, nah, she ain't got no sister. She got some cousins, though. You ain't see 'em with her last night? They were there."

"Man, I was so faded, I don't remember shit."

"Aw well, they'll be where we're headed to now," lil' bro informed him.

"Damn right, bet. A nigga tryna buss something DOWN! Especially if they looking like her." Maniac rubbed his hands together like Birdman.

"Ole goofy ass!" I shot, glancing at him through the rearview mirror.

"Nigga, fuck you!" he grimaced before blowing a thick cloud of smoke towards the front of my ride.

Just like Menace, Maniac was like a brother to us. His grandmother stayed next door to us when we were little. We'd gotten cool after one of our homeboys tried to punk him for his bike, and Maniac whooped the dog shit out of him. As the years went on, we became family.

"Aye, speaking of her cousins – where you and Rhymedi dip off to last night?" Havoc asked, looking over at me.

"None of your fuckin' business, nigga," I replied.

"Mmh, yeah aight," he snickered. "You hit that, didn't you?"

"Nigga, what?!" I looked at his ass sideways.

"Man, why you getting all swole in the chest? If you hit it, you hit it."

"Fuck out of here, bruh." I couldn't do shit but laugh at his clown ass. "Ain't nobody HIT shit," I then stated honestly.

"Then where y'all go?"

"Bruh! Why does it matter? Why the fuck you clockin' what I'm doing?"

"Same reason you be clocking the bitches I'm fuckin'. Yo' ass be the main one preaching about fuckin' on the first night. Damn hypocrite."

"Nigga, shut the fuck up. I just told yo' dumb ass I didn't fuck," I sneered.

"Aight, cool. So, what y'all leave the club to do? Go to Bible study?" he asked, causing Menace and Maniac to bust a chuckle.

Shaking my head, I sucked my teeth in annoyance. This dude never took anything seriously. Everything had to be a fuckin' joke to him. It wasn't his business what me and Rhymedi left the club for. Yet, he insisted on pressing the issue.

"If you must know, we went to grab a bite to eat, talked a little bit, and I took her back to the house," I lied.

He didn't need to know why we'd left early. What had taken place last night was solely between Rhymedi and I, and it was going to stay that way. If she wanted anyone to know what happened, she would have to tell them herself.

"Awww shit, okay. I see what type of time you on," Havoc chuckled. "You like her, huh?"

Scoffing, I cracked a slight smile. "I mean, she cool as hell. Plus, she's beautiful as fuck. I guess you can say I'm feeling shorty," I shrugged.

"Nigga, you don't GUESS shit! Ole babe got yo' ass smitten as hell. Look at you, blushing and shit." Maniac put my ass on blast.

"Man, gone with that bullshit. Ain't nobody blushing," I stated, while still grinning.

"It's all good, big bro. If you like her, you like her. At least this one can't run out yo' life like Ariel did," he cracked, causing everyone to laugh but me.

"On my mama, yo' bitch ass going to hell, boy!" Menace was laughing so hard, he had tears in his eyes.

"Shit, his ass IS hell," Maniac added.

"The nigga ain't even fuckin' funny," I sucked my teeth. "Ole clown ass," I then grimaced.

"I'm just fuckin' around, bro; I apologize, damn! Chill the fuck out; it was just a lil' jokey joke. I had to get that one off – it was perfect timing, bro," he snickered.

"Yeah, whatever, bitch," I shot, getting off the interstate at our exit.

Five minutes later, we were pulling up to our beach property. Hopping out, I grabbed one cooler while Havoc grabbed the other. Menace and Maniac grabbed the other shit we'd brought along — sides, beach props, ice and some more shit. Approaching the door, I rang the bell. I could've just punched in the code since it was our shit, but it was only right to keep it respectful. The ladies could've still been getting dressed or some other shit.

Seconds later, Monica let us in. "Heeey, Homicide, Havoc; what's up?" she beamed brightly, stepping to the side.

"'Sup, Monica," I stated.

"What it do, Lips?" Havoc shot her a head nod.

Scoffing, she let out a light snicker. "Really? Just like that, huh? I swear, I can't stand yo' ass!" she spat, shaking her head in shame. "Ooooh, who is this y'all brought with y'all?" She then asked as Menace and Maniac entered the threshold.

Chortling at her reaction, Maniac also gave her a head nod. "What up, miss lady? Maniac's the name," he introduced himself, causing her to flash a wide smile.

"Ooooh, and he has an accent," she hiked her brows. "Monica, nice to meet you. I'll be sure to catch up with you later," she giggled, blowing him a kiss.

Chuckling, Menace shook his head. "Mmm, I see she already choosing. What's up, shorty? I'm –,"

"Menace," she turned up her top lip, cutting him off. "I remember your arrogant ass from last night," she spat, causing us all to fall out laughing.

"**BOW! BOW! BOW!**" Maniac made gunshot noises. "Just shot that nigga the fuck down!"

"SOMEOME PLEASE CALL 911!" Havoc added in Wyclef's voice.

"On God, fuck y'all!" Menace sucked his teeth. "And fuck you too, shorty," he looked at Monica up and down. "That's why I got more money than that nigga," he chuckled, brushing past her.

"Yeah aight!" Maniac yelled from the kitchen.

Shaking her head in shame, Monica snickered as she closed and locked the door behind us. After informing us that she was going to get the rest of the girls, she disappeared into another part of the house. While she did that, Havoc got the grill going as I got the meat ready for him. Menace and Maniac set up the volleyball net and other games.

When the ladies showed up in the kitchen, I couldn't help but notice that my lil' boo, Rhymedi, wasn't with them. Curious to know why, I nodded for her cousin to come holler at me.

"What's up, bro? Oooh, that meat smells so good, and it ain't even cooked yet," she giggled, rubbing her belly.

"Yeeeaahh, that's how you know this shit 'bout to be on point," I chuckled, nodding confidently.

"Lawd, I can't wait," she shook her head, licking her lips.

"Yo' ass silly as fuck," I told her. "But off subject, where's Rhymedi?"

Letting out a heavy breath, she shook her head in disappointment. "She's back there in the room, still mad about last night. I brought her lunch earlier, and she refused to accept it – right before reading my ass for filth," she smacked her lips and rolled her eyes.

"What?! Why? What's she mad at you for?"

"For leaving her," Brittani sneered, sucking her teeth. "She claims we turned our backs on her."

"What? Aw nah – it wasn't even like that."

Brittani smacked her lips again. "See, that's what the fuck I'm saying. I even told her that, but she wasn't trying to hear it. And it's killing me because I love the fuck out of my cousin. I would never intentionally turn my back on her." Her eyes watered as her feelings rolled off of her tongue. "Homicide, I brought her on this trip to show her a good time, and now I just feel like I've ruined everything." A tear managed to escape, but she swiftly wiped it away.

"It's all good, sis, don't trip. I'm about to go holler at her and see what's up, aight?"

"Kay, thanks, bro."

"None needed. Just do me a favor and put that meat in the pan and take it out to lil' bro for me."

"Alright, I got you," she assured me.

Leaving her in the kitchen, I made my way to the master suite – where Rhymedi was staying. I approached the closed door and gave it three firm taps. When she didn't answer, I repeated the method.

"Go away," I heard her vaguely, causing me to knock again. "I SAID, GO AWAY!" she then screamed, causing me to scrunch my face. Turning the nob, I politely let myself in. I didn't know who she thought she was yelling at, but her ass was going to learn to tighten that shit up.

"Aye shorty, who you talking to?" I asked calmly, but sternly enough for her to know I was serious.

Noticing it was me, Rhymedi's face went from hard to soft in a matter of seconds. Her eyes darted to the floor, and she gave the expression of a scared toddler. Clenching my jaws together, I sucked my teeth in annoyance. I hated when she did that type of shit. It showed her insecurities, and I didn't like that.

"Homicide – what are you doing here?" she murmured, fidgeting with her fingernails.

"I'm up here, ma. Look at me," I told her, causing her to spring her head up immediately. "You always look a muthafucka in the eyes when you're talking to them. You ain't beneath no fuckin' body, aight?" I told her, meaning every word.

"Yes," she mumbled.

"Say what?"

"Yes, I hear you." She spoke a little louder.

"Nah, it's yes, big daddy," I barked.

Exhaling heavily, she gave me the side eye. "Yes bi –"

"Girl, you ain't gotta say that shit. I'm just fuckin' around," I chuckled, causing her to crack a slight smile.

Shaking her head, she rolled her eyes to the top of her head. "I swear, you play too much. What is it that you want, sir?" she then asked me.

"You," I answered without hesitation.

The room fell silent as Rhymedi and I shared an intense stare. For the first time ever, a nigga caught butterflies in the pit of my stomach. Tucking my bottom lip between my teeth, I walked closer in her space. I could hear her breaths pick up with each step I took. Lowering her head, her eyes slowly landed towards the floor again.

"What's wrong, shorty?" I asked, placing two fingers underneath her chin, softly lifting her head until her eyes met mine. "I make you uncomfortable?"

Her eyes danced around a bit before falling back on me. Rubbing her palms against her thighs, she slowly shrugged. "I wouldn't say uncomfortable, but do you make me nervous? Yes," she finally admitted, biting into her bottom lip.

"Why I make you nervous?"

"I don't know; you just do," she lightly blushed, shaking her head.

"Calm down, shorty. I'm a good guy; ain't no need to be nervous when you're with me. Aight?" I stated sincerely as I looked in her eyes.

"Kay," she simply uttered, surprisingly keeping eye contact.

This girl was so damn beautiful, the shit should be a crime. I wanted to lean over and kiss her in her in the mouth, but I didn't want to cross no boundaries. There was a time and place for everything, and we weren't there just yet. I still had some hurdles to cross before we took that next step.

"So why you locked up in here? The party's out there," I nodded my head towards the door.

Rhymedi slowly shrugged as that sad look reappeared. "I don't know, I'm just not feeling it. I'd rather sit in here and look out at the water; it's more peaceful," she stated.

"Why just look when we could be out there?" I questioned with a raised brow.

Smacking her lips, Rhymedi rolled her eyes with a grimace. "I could've sworn we've been through this already," she spat. "How the fuck am I supposed to get out there?" her nostrils flared in frustration.

"Aye, chill all that shit out. Didn't I just tell you about that aggressive ass shit when I first walked in? You too fuckin' pretty for that shit. If I'm treating you good, I expect the same in return – aight?"

Swallowing hard, she looked up at me. "Understood. I apologize," she stated sincerely. "But the question still stands. How am I supposed to get out there?"

"That wasn't the question, though, was it?" I cocked my head to the side. "I asked, why just look when we can go out? Now, do you wanna go out or not?"

Clicking her tongue against the roof of her mouth, she pursed her lips. "Sure, Homicide, I would love to," she softly giggled.

"Now how hard was that? Ole mean ass," I chucked. "I'ma nickname yo' ass sour patch."

"Whatever, "she snickered. "You better come on before I change my mind," she then told me.

"Yeah aight," I sighed, sucking my teeth. "I see yo' lil' ass wanna learn the hard way," I stated, causing her to snicker.

Swiftly scooping her up into my arms bridal style, I walked out the balcony door and onto the beach. I got as close to the shore as possible before gently placing her down in the sand. She used her arms to prop herself up. Digging her toes into the sand, Rhymedi stared out into the distance as the sunset beamed off of her beautiful, mocha-colored complextion. By the mild expression displayed on her face, I could tell something was on her mind. Taking a seat behind her, I pulled her back against my chest before coddling her in my arms.

"What's on your mind, beautiful?" I then asked, interlocking her fingers with mine. Exhaling lightly, she shook her head. "Yes, it is; I can tell. Now talk to me."

"I just can't remember the last time I've felt this at peace," she finally admitted.

"What you mean?"

"I mean, for the past year, my life has been a mess," she scoffed, still staring out at the water. "I've been in a really dark place. Being in this chair has brought out the worst in me. To be honest, I'm just over life. I don't see how God allowed this to happen to me." She sniffled, and I noticed tears slowly rolling down her cheeks.

"So, you blame God for this happening to you?" I asked, curiously.

Sneering, she smacked her lips. "Who else is there to blame? I mean, He is the ruler of all things – or am I wrong?"

"True, but he would never do anything to hurt us. At least, I don't believe so," I stated honestly. "But I will tell you what I know for a fact is true."

"And what's that?"

"Everything happens for a reason, and no one is exempt from anything. It could be me in a chair; that's why you don't take shit for granted and live every day like it's your last," I preached. "You may be in a chair, Rhymedi, but you aren't dead. Meaning, you still have another chance to do everything your heart desires."

There was an awkward silence as I continued to hold Rhymedi in my arms, while she stared out at the water. I could tell what I'd just said to her was weighing heavy on her mind. Life had traumatized shorty, leaving her broken, bitter, and clueless. I hoped she would allow me to help her change that. There was still so much life had to offer Rhymedi; yet, she was letting that chair hold her back from experiencing it.

"If I told you I wanted to take you on a date before y'all catch flight tomorrow, would you let me?" I questioned, breaking the silence.

"Uhm, I guess," she shrugged.

"Nah, ain't no you guess. It's a yes or no question." I gently grabbed her chin, turning her face to meet mine. "Now, will you like to spend the morning with me before you leave to go back home?" I resubmitted the question.

"Yes, I would love that," she smiled, sealing the deal.

"Alright, then it's a date." I bit into my bottom lip as I stared into her eyes.

Rhymedi and I sat on the beach a little while longer, enjoying the breeze and making small talk. Once we were done enjoying one another, I carried her back in, and we made our way to the kitchen to enjoy time with the rest of the gang.

# *Rhymedi*

"Oh my gosh, Rhymedi, you look so beautiful!" Brittani complimented as she put the finishing touches on my makeup.

She was helping me get ready for my date with Homicide. It was our last few hours in California; we were scheduled to board the jet by noon.

"Thanks to you," I smiled, looking up at Britt. "I love you, cousin," I stated sincerely.

"Awww stink, I love you toooo!" she leaned over, hugging me tightly around the neck. "You know you're my boo." She placed a kiss onto my cheek.

"I know," I grabbed her hand, squeezing it. "That's why I want to apologize for being a bitch to you. You haven't done anything but be here for me in my time of need. You didn't deserve the way I treated you yesterday. I was just so angry, and I didn't have anyone to take it out on, so I took it out on you guys," I sighed, shaking my head in shame. "I sincerely apologize for my actions, and I hope you can forgive me."

"Girl," Brittani smacked her lips, lightly nudging me in the arm. "There's nothing to forgive; I was never upset. No offense, but I never take your temper tantrums to heart. Not because I don't care, but because I sympathize with you. It has to be hard having to adjust to a whole new lifestyle in the blink of an eye —being able to walk and do everything on your own one day, to being confined to a chair the next. That's some traumatic ass shit! I may not know how you feel, cousin, but I can imagine, and I sympathize with you. But just know as long as I have breath in my body, I will always be here for you," she finished, and I was all choked up.

"Thank you. Thank you for everything – especially this trip. It was everything I didn't know I needed. I got to experience things I never thought I'd experience, and I met a man I thought would never be into me. Bitch, I can't believe I'm really about to go on a date with Homicide's fine, rich ass!" I had butterflies just thinking about it.

"And why the fuck not?" Brittani scoffed, folding her arms across her chest. "Rhymedi, you are one dope ass person. You're beautiful, sweet, smart, and a whole fuckin' vibe. I'll be glad when you stop sleeping on yourself and realize that," she told me, causing a few tears to trickle from my eyes.

"Oh, no ma'am! See, that's what we're NOT about to do," she stated quickly, snatching tissues from the box on the bathroom sink, patting my face dry. "I spent a whole hour on this makeup. I'll be damned if you fuck up this beat!" she chuckled.

"I'm sorry! It's just all this mushy shit is getting to a bitch," I giggled.

"Oh damn, my bad. I was getting a little too sentimental, huh?"

"Uh, duh!" We both fell out laughing.

***Ding, Dong!***

We heard the bell, and I knew Homicide had arrived. It was confirmed when Alicia's big mouth ass called out to me.

"Rhym! Your knight in shining armor is here!" she yelled, skipping up the hallway. When she finally made it into the bathroom, her bottom jaw hit the floor. "Oooooh bitch, you is fine as hell!" she smiled from ear to ear. "MONICA! Monica, come look at Rhymedi!"

"Bitch, why the hell is you yelling like a damn foo –," Monica's words got caught in her throat when her eyes landed on me. Throwing her hands over her mouth, her eyes watered. "Awwww

Rhym, you look so gorgeous. I mean, you always look good, but you look GOODT right now. Britt, you definitely did that! And that dress looks painted on, honey!" she snapped, referring to the short, red body con dress that hugged my slim-thick figure. "Let me find out you tryna get some cuddy before we leave!" Monica hiked her brow in suspicion.

"Let's just say, I ain't ducking NO action!" I snickered.

"Okaaaay! Now that's what the fuck I'm talking about!" Alicia slapped fives with me.

"Oh lord, y'all just some freaks!" Brittani added, shaking her head.

"Uh un, don't do that, bitch. 'Cause we heard you and Havoc all last night 'til the wee hours of the morning," Alicia busted her out.

"Ooooh cousin, and she ain't lyin'," Monica added with a sour expression. "Y'all was loud too."

"Real loud," I added, scratching the back of my neck.

"See, now – uh un!" Brittani popped her lips. "Y'all in my business, and I don't like that," she playfully rolled her eyes. "Besides, it's not about me right now; it's about Rhym. Now, if you'll excuse me, my bro is waiting, and we have a schedule to keep." Brittani finished unlocking the wheels of my chair, proceeding to push me towards the front of the beach house.

When we made it to the living room, Homicide was sitting on the couch, looking good as ever, with a dozen pink roses occupying his left hand. Standing to his feet, he licked his lips as his eyes roamed over my appearance.

"Good lord, girl," he chuckled, tugging at his beard. "Are we going to breakfast, or you trying to be the breakfast?" He leaned down and placed a gentle kiss onto my forehead. "These are for you, beautiful." He then handed me the roses.

Blushing, I stuck my nose into them, inhaling the fresh

scent. "Thank you, they're so pretty," I beamed from ear to ear.

"You ready for a morning you'll never forget?"

"As a matter of fact, I am," I replied confidently, looking up at him.

"Say no more," he winked, flashing his perfect, white smile.

"Alright, I'll help you get her to the car." Brittani commenced to rolling me out the front door, until he stopped her.

"Ayo sis, no disrespect, but I got this," he chortled, softly nudging her out of the way. "When I offered to take her on this date, I offered to accept everything that comes along with it," he told her sincerely.

"Oh, well, excuse the hell of me," Britt chuckled, throwing her hands up in surrender. "Do ya thang, brother."

Taking over, Homicide pushed me towards his truck with my cousin in tow. After placing the lock on my chair, he opened the door, picked me up, and placed me in the passenger's seat. Once snapping my seatbelt around me, he proceeded to fold my chair up and put it in the back. I snickered as I watched Brittani looking on to make sure he did everything properly. The girl was like a drill Sargent, but I loved every bit of her overprotectiveness.

"You sure you're going to be okay? You know I'll tag along if you want me to," she told me as Homicide closed the back door of the truck.

"No, you don't have to. I'm good, I promise," I smiled, grabbing ahold of her hand.

"Okay, I'm just checking. Have fun and I love you. I'm just a phone call away if you need anything."

"Kay, I love you too. See you in a minute." I blew her an air kiss.

"In a minute," Britt smiled, doing the same. "Homicide, take care of my cousin or I'll –,"

"Fuck me up," he finished her statement hopping into the driver's seat, cranking the engine. "I know, sis, we've been here before. She's good, I got her – I promise."

"Alright, as long as you know what's up," she giggled. "Y'all have fun and don't do anything I wouldn't do," she winked, closing me in.

Standing in the doorway, Brittani watched us until we were out of sight.

∞ ∞ ∞

About thirty minutes later, we were pulling up to a beautiful, high-rise building. Placing the truck in park, Homicide hopped out and got me together. He tipped valet after giving him the keys and a head nod. Pushing me into the building, I was in awe of how beautiful it was. As we approached the elevator and he pressed the upward arrow, I could feel butterflies swarming in the pit of my stomach as I anticipated what was to come. Getting on, I got even more nervous when I'd noticed he pressed the highest number, which was twenty-four. I was terrified of heights, but I refused to tell him that. I didn't want to ruin what he had planned.

Finally arriving to our designated floor, the elevator doors opened. My bottom jaw hit the floor when my eyes landed on the beautiful ass penthouse before me. There was a trail of red rose petals, beginning right in front of the elevator exit. Pushing me forward, Homicide proceeded to follow them. When it led us out onto the balcony to a beautifully decorated table for two, I gasped in astonishment.

"Oh my gosh! This is so beautiful!" My eyes watered as I cupped my hands over my mouth.

Chuckling, Homicide pushed my chair to the table. "It's just a little something – nothing major. I guess it'll do for it being last minute, though, huh?" he stated, placing the lock on my wheels, before walking around and taking a seat in the chair across from me.

Smacking my lips, I waved him off. "I don't care what you say, this looks amazing, and the food looks great!" I replied, gazing over all of the scrumptious looking selections.

There was everything — from fluffy Belgian waffles, deep fried lobster tails, shrimp and grits, fried potatoes, and thick cut bacon, to pastries, fruit, champagne, and freshly squeezed orange juice. A bitch couldn't wait to dig in. Though I was tiny, I was a big girl at heart – food made me happy.

"I know this is a lot of food, but I didn't know what you liked, so I had my chef whip up some of everything. I hope I didn't go overboard," Homicide chuckled as we both prepared our plates.

"Well, you sure your chef doesn't know me personally? Because he prepared EVERYTHING I like," I giggled. "To be honest, I just like food. It's the key to my heart," I told him.

"Oh, well, in that case, I've unlocked it then, huh?" he peered at me sexily.

Blushing, I bit a piece of my bacon. Homicide was laying his charm on thick, **and not falling for him was becoming hard.** It had only been three days, and he'd reeled me in like a fish on a hook line. I was beyond smitten with this man — so smitten, that I was beginning to dread having to leave to go back home. It had been months since I'd been in the presence of a man. So, being in the presence of one of Homicide's caliber, hit different. He was like a breath of fresh air.

"What you over there thinking about?" Homicide asked, breaking me from my thoughts.

It was if his ass had known me forever. He could always tell something was on my mind without me even having to say it. Grabbing a napkin, I wiped my mouth and shrugged.

"Just life,"

"Oh yeah? What about it? How beautiful you're going to look barefoot and pregnant on our wedding day?" he asked, causing me to bust a chuckle.

"What? You can't be serious right now. I think we're jumping just a little too far ahead," I giggled.

"Nah, I'm just fuckin' around," he chortled. "But seriously, tell me what's on your mind." He grabbed the champagne and proceeded to pour up two mimosas.

"Just thinking about how funny life works. I never thought I would ever be in the presence of another man. Just this time last year, I was trying to get over a major heartbreak," I scoffed before taking a sip of my mimosa. "The man I planned on spending the rest of my life with, walked out to go to the store one day and never returned. We had been together four long years – he'd proposed the night we'd gotten into the accident that landed me in this chair. When we were told that I would no longer be able to walk again, he switched up in the blink of an eye, started treating me like shit, verbally abusing me," I sniffled as a few tears trickled down my cheeks. Just telling Homicide my story made the events playback in my mind.

Clearing my throat, I patted my eyes dry with a napkin. "Anyway, I vowed that I would never let another man in because the one I planned on spending the rest of my life with, left me when I needed him most," I shrugged nonchalantly.

Getting up from his seat, Homicide walked over and kneeled down in front of me. He placed his finger underneath my chin and softly lifted my face to make me look at him.

"As I told you last night, shorty, everything happens for a reason. It was destined for that nigga to be out of your life, so that you could meet me. He wasn't built for the lifestyle God has planned for you, but a man like me, is. I adore you, Rhymedi. Just last week, the woman I was supposed to marry walked out on me for another man, and I was crushed. But when I laid eyes on you that night at the club, I knew God had better plans for me," he stated, causing me to chuckle.

"Wait, what? Are you serious?"

"Dead ass! Straight left me for some Pat Saijak ass dude."

"No way! A white man?" my mouth hung open in shock.

"I can't make this shit up."

"Woooow, that's crazy. I'm sorry to hear that," I sympathized with him.

Scoffing, he chortled. "For what? Now that I'm here with you, I'm happy she left. Her ass wasn't any good for me anyway; I was just tying to convince myself she was because I loved her."

"Yeah," I sighed. "I know exactly how that goes," I agreed.

"But something tells me I don't have to worry about that with you. I know for a fact you're good for me." He tucked his bottom lip between his teeth, gazing at me like dinner on a Sunday after church.

"Oh yeah? And just how do you know that?" I questioned right above a whisper.

"Because I know." He slowly roamed my body with his eyes. "You look good, smell good. I bet you taste good, too," he licked his lips.

My heart palpitated, and my coochie quivered as the scent of Creed mixed with the champagne on his breath engulfed my nostrils. This man was driving me crazy, yet he hadn't even touched my ass, and that's what scared me. Men who could do that type of shit were dangerous.

Homicide leaned in and placed his soft ass lips on top of mine. Slipping his tongue into my mouth, I welcomed him as he kissed me passionately. "Can I taste you, Rhymedi?" His words vibrated off of my lips as he continued to kiss me.

"Yes," I whispered, ready for whatever he had to offer.

Breaking our lip-lock, Homicide stood to his feet, swiftly

knocking everything on the table, off. He picked me up from my chair, gently sitting me on the edge. Using my arms to hold myself up, I watched as he slid his hands up my dress and removed my panties. Homicide then mounted himself between my legs, kissing and biting up both of my thighs. My head rolled back in blessedness as he latched onto my clit with his lips.

"Oooh, fuck!" I gasped as he swirled the tip of his tongue around my pearl in a circular motion.

The warmness of his mouth felt so good against my pussy. It had been so long since I'd been touched sexually, I'd forgotten what the shit felt like – but Homicide was the perfect reminder.

Slowly running my fingers through the parts of his cornrows, I pushed his head deeper into my honey pot. I didn't know why I'd chosen to do that because it sent his ass into overdrive. He began slurping the pussy like an Icee on a hot, summer day.

"Oooh Homicide, you're about to make this pussy cum!" I cried, biting into my bottom lip.

"Let that shit loose!" he demanded, sucking my now protruding clit harder.

He even went as far as slipping two fingers into my tunnel. Moving them in and out, I felt a tingling sensation, and I knew I was about to reach my peak.

"Oh my gosh, baby, here it comes. Ooooh, it's cummimg!" I screamed before the flood gates opened, squirting all over his face. It was so much, his beard and the collar of his shirt were soaking wet.

"Damn shorty, that's how you coming?" he chuckled, removing his shirt and using it to wipe his mouth.

"Oh my gosh, I'm so sorry."

Collapsing back onto the table, I threw my hands over my face in shame. It had been months since I'd had an orgasm, and

T'ANN MARIE

Homicide had just caught all my backed up fluids.

# Homicide

"Damn shorty, you're really about to leave a nigga," I chortled, looking down at Rhymedi as we were alongside the jet, preparing for them to board.

Our wonderful morning had dreadfully come to an end, and now it was time for her to head back home. It was killing me to see her go. We'd become so close in such a short amount of time, it had a nigga contemplating extending her stay.

"I know, right," she pouted. "Just a few days ago, I didn't even want to come; now, I don't want to leave. Funny how things change so quickly, huh?" she giggled, shaking her head.

There was an awkward silence as she and I stared at one another. I began to get that butterfly feeling in the pit of my stomach again. It had only been three days, and she was already pulling at my heart strings. She had a nigga ready to alter his whole lifestyle just to be with her ass. This shit was wild.

"You know you don't have to go, right?" I told her, taking her hands into mine.

"Awww," she smiled, batting her beautiful ass eyes at me. "As much as I would love to, I can't. I gotta get back to work," she finished, causing me to smack my teeth.

"Fuck that job, shorty. I got you," I chuckled.

"And as nice as that sounds, let's be real," she chortled, cocking her head to the side. "You're a busy man, with multiple businesses. I require a lot, Homicide, and I refuse to disrupt everything you got going on. I can't be that burden." She dropped her eyes towards the ground.

Sucking my teeth, I gently grabbed her chin and raised her head back up. "Aye, what I tell you about that shit, shorty? Shit don't change just because you're going back home. Keep your eyes forward and head up at all times, you hear me?" I stared at her straight in the eyes. Rhymedi's eyes watered as she nodded. "And as far as this being a burden shit, I bet not ever hear you say that again. Yes, you require more attention than most – so what? That doesn't make you any less valuable than the next woman. I'm a grown ass man who can handle anything that comes my way. I ain't your ex-man; I'm the best man, never forget that," I told her, meaning every word.

Sighing, Rhymedi let out a slight giggle. "You always know just what to say. You're too good to be true, you know that?"

"Nah, I got flaws too, shorty. I'm just a real ass nigga," I replied honestly.

I wasn't no perfect ass nigga, and I didn't portray to be, but I knew how a woman was supposed to be treated. I had compassion for the next human, and I handled people how I wanted to be handled – with care.

Smiling up at me, Rhymedi gazed into my eyes. "Thank you so much, Homicide. This weekend has been nothing short of amazing, and it's all because of you."

"No thanks needed, shorty. You deserved it all and more. You have my number, so I'm expecting you to stay in touch. Don't go back to St. Louis and forget about a nigga," I told her.

"I would never," she snickered. "Believe it or not, you're pretty unforgettable," she smiled, making a nigga's heart flutter.

"Taking off in five, boss!" my pilot warned, walking past us.

"Aight, bet," I nodded. Sighing heavily, I focused my attention back on Rhymedi. "Well, I guess we better get you boarded, huh?"

"Yeah, I guess so," Rhymedi smiled.

Bending forward, I scooped her up into my arms and proceeded up the stairs of the jet. When we made it on, Havoc and the rest of the ladies were sitting around, chatting over champagne.

"It's about damn time. Fuck y'all was out there talking about?" Havoc asked as I gently placed Rhymedi down in her seat.

"Right, I wanna know too," Brittani popped her lips.

"Uh un, y'all in my business, don't do that," Rhymedi giggled.

"Exactly, nosey asses," I chuckled, shaking my head in shame. "Anyway, have a safe trip, shorty, and don't forget what I told you." I focused my attention back on Rhymedi.

"Kay, I won't. Promise," she replied, staring into my eyes.

Before I could even think about it, our lips collided. Grabbing ahold of both sides of my face, Rhymedi deepened the kiss. As our tongues danced around, I could've sworn a nigga saw fireworks, causing the kiss to last a lot longer than expected.

"Damn, nigga! You gon' let her breathe or nah?" Havoc spat, causing everyone to bust out laughing. Without interrupting our passionate lip-lock, I flipped his hating ass the bird. He always had some clown shit to say.

About thirty seconds later, our kiss finally came to an end. "Call me when you land and get situated," I then told Rhymedi, slowly running my thumb down the center of her chin.

"Will do," she simply uttered, still mesmerized.

"Alright ladies, nice meeting you all and until next time," I saluted.

"Byyyee!" they all replied in unison.

Havoc and Brittani said their final goodbyes before we exited the aircraft. Standing off to the side of the takeoff strip, I watched all the way up until they were in the air. I glanced over and noticed my little brother staring at me with a silly ass grin on his face.

"What, bitch?" I sneered, looking at him out the corner of my eyes.

"Yo' ass done got a piece of that paraplegic pussy and it got yo' head gone," he chuckled, shaking his head.

Sucking my teeth, I couldn't do shit but laugh at the nigga. "I swear, mama dropped you on yo' head as a baby, boy – you fucked up. Bring yo' stupid ass on," I chuckled, heading for my ride.

Little did his silly ass know, I hadn't even hit. Rhymedi wasn't the kind of girl you just fucked and sent on her way – she was way too special for that. Nevertheless, I did leave something on her mind to remember a nigga by.

# *Rhymedi*

## *One Week Later*

"Oh my gosh, ma, this is so good! Why haven't you told me about this place sooner?" I asked, stuffing my face with seafood dip.

We were out dining at this new black owned restaurant by the name of Gulf Shore. Well, it wasn't that new, but it was new to me.

"Hell, when did I have the chance? Your butt was so set on never leaving the house again, I couldn't get you hip," she replied, taking a sip from her water.

"Really, ma? Cut it out," I snickered.

"What? Ain't that what y'all say? Get me hip," she chuckled, mocking the slang we used.

"Oh lord, ma, please stop."

"Why I gotta stop? I'm just trying to keep up with what's in. What, I'm too old for that?"

"Definitely," I nodded, just teasing.

"Girl, please. I can run with the best of them, and my knees still work like Megan Thee Stallion. I know you shame!"

"Oh my gosh, maaaa!" I gasped, looking around the restaurant, making sure no one had heard her. I couldn't believe her ass was really in public clowning like this. "I can't take you right now. You're something else, you know that, right?"

"Girl shit, that's how I stay young. Ain't no fun in being a damn stick in the mud."

"That part," I hiked my brows, taking a sip of my margarita.

It had been a week since my trip to Calabasas, and life couldn't have been better. As promised, I'd been keeping in touch with Homicide. We talked just about every day on FaceTime. On the days we didn't talk, we were texting. We were even making plans for him to come visit in the near future. Though we hadn't placed a title on anything, it was safe to say he was Bae. I was his person, and he was mine. The bond we were building was one I'd never experienced. Not only was he making me fall in love with him, but he was teaching me how to love myself again. He spoke life into me, something no man had done – other than my father. He was the best thing I never knew I needed, and I had my cousin to thank for that. If you asked me, our spring break getaway didn't owe me a damn thing!

"So, I was thinking. When we leave here, we should go to the mall. Macy's got a sale, and I could use a little retail therapy," I suggested, popping another chip coated with dip into my mouth.

"Excuse me? Say what now?" my mother asked, making sure she'd heard me correctly.

"Ma, stop playing. You heard me," I giggled.

"Lunch and the mall?" she asked with a raised brow. "Who is this new woman before me?"

Giggling, I took another sip of my drink. "There's nothing new, ma," I smiled. "I just think it's time I get back to the old me. You know, the Rhymedi before this chair," I winked.

THE END….

# Join Our Mailing List:

http://eepurl.com/gU81k5